How I Killed
Margaret Thatcher

Also by Anthony Cartwright

The Afterglow
Heartland

How I Killed
Margaret Thatcher

Anthony Cartwright

**Tindal
Street
Press**

First published in 2012
by Tindal Street Press Ltd
217 The Custard Factory, Gibb Street, Birmingham, B9 4AA
www.tindalstreet.co.uk

A CIP catalogue reference for this book is available
from the British Library

ISBN: 978 1 906994 35 8

Typeset by Tetragon

Printed and bound in Great Britain
by CPI Group (UK) Ltd, Croydon, CR0 4YY

Judas Iscariot's here, look. Here comes Judas Iscariot.

My grandad says this as my uncle Eric walks up the path from the allotments. He smiles and it sounds like he's joking, but even from this distance I can see that my grandad's eyes are like the crocodile's at the zoo.

All right, Jack, Uncle Eric says and looks confused.

My grandad walks right up to him and says Judas again and then lamps Uncle Eric in the face and knocks him across the back steps. I have never seen anything like this before in my life. Last Sunday they had their arms around each other in the front room, singing I'll take you home again, Kathleen; now they're wrestling on the steps. I have never seen grown-ups have a fight, let alone my own grandad. He's fifty-six years old. My nan screams, so does my mum; so does Stella, my uncle Eric's daughter, and she tries to pull my grandad back. Uncle Eric is bigger and younger than my grandad; my nan says that when Uncle Eric wears his sunglasses at the caravans he looks like Roy Orbison.

My grandad is off him now, on his feet, out of breath. He points through the back gate and down the path through the allotments.

Never come here again. Never come to this house again. Dun yer hear me?

My grandad spits on the ground. My nan says his name, Jack, Jack, Jack. Stella looks at her broken fingernails. Uncle Eric scrambles up to his feet and goes back the way he came. My grandad points.

Dyer hear me, Judas?

I have never seen anything like this in my life.

She tried to kill me, after all. She tried to kill all of us. I nearly died on her first day as prime minister. I fell out of that back bedroom window at my nan and grandad's house just after the fight. I used to sit on the window ledge and look out across the allotments, at my grandad strolling between the pyramids built for runner beans and sweet peas and the bright coloured windmills that were meant to scare the birds; at Cleopatra, the Robertsons' sand-coloured cat, still as a sphinx on the fence, and at all the factories and works yards beyond. I lost my balance, tumbled off my perch, after the most incredible thing I had ever seen in my life; grunting and swearing, the radio playing at the same time, almost teatime; my mum sat at the kitchen table waiting for my dad to come back from work.

I flipped over in mid-air, saw all the chimneys in the distance, smoke dripping slowly into the sky; and then came upright, and then upside-down again, then halfway between. And that probably saved my life because I went arse-first through the shed roof, with a crash like a bomb going off.

I remember I thought I was dead. This is what it's like to be dead and gone, I thought, all the air knocked out of me, looking up at the outline I'd made in the roof, the shape of a nine-year-old boy, that I thought was maybe my soul ascending. Perhaps I didn't think that then, but I understood that when you died you left your body and went somewhere else and I thought I'd get to see my great-granny and my grandad's pet budgie, Jennie Lee. Jennie Lee was named after Nye Bevan's wife, my grandad would explain to people and watch for their reaction. He'd recently found her stiff and lifeless on the bottom of the birdcage. And although I realized I'd miss everyone, I supposed I'd see them all soon enough so it didn't matter that much.

In fact, I'd been saved by my own backside and a big pile of dust sheets left by the council after they'd decorated the downstairs room for my great-granny to stay in before she died.

When the air rushed back into my lungs, I let out a scream that my mum said later was exactly the same as the one I gave when I was born. My arse felt like it was on fire; my lungs like they were sucking in air from one of the furnaces that used to blink and glow out in the distance when it got dark.

My grandad thumped Uncle Eric because he voted for Margaret Thatcher and pretended not to have. I don't know how my grandad found out; voting's supposed to be secret. I hadn't even heard the name Margaret Thatcher until a few days ago and I'm already sick of it. I'm worried too because I know there's a bigger secret to come out. My dad voted for her as well. He voted Conservative, Tory, which is the same thing. I'm not meant to know but I overheard him tell my mum.

Oh, Francis. What yer done that for, yer saft devil? she asked him.

When she said that it wasn't like when she says it for things like when he's left wet towels lying on the floor or that time he gave a five pound note to Natalie Robertson when it was her birthday and my mum thought it was too much to give her; no, her voice was sad and heavy when she said it and I knew it was something bad.

My dad didn't say anything, shrugged his shoulders. He wasn't meant to have voted for her. My mum told him he was wrong, that he'd made a mistake and not to say anything else about it, for God's sake. We're all Labour. Our MP's Labour: my dad's vote didn't really count; or my uncle Eric's. They made a mistake, I suppose.

I supposed it then and I suppose it even more now. I worried about what would happen if my grandad ever found out about my dad, a worry that ebbed and flowed for years afterwards. It was only when it was too late that I realized we had other things to worry about.

My uncle Eric died a few years ago; he was on holiday in Benidorm and had a heart attack. They had to fly the body back. He and aunty Sheila were making plans to move out there. Eric had done all right for himself, set up a scaffolding firm, got a contract from the council. I went to the funeral. My grandad stayed at home, refused to come to his own brother's funeral. I sat in the car with Stella. She comes in the pub every few Sundays when we do a roast dinner. We never mention the feud.

There are faces above me, familiar and terrified, my mum and nan; Stella, whose mascara runs across her face as she cries; and my best mate, Little Ronnie Robertson, who has scrambled over the fence from next door at the sound of the crash, his glasses wonky like always. His sisters are in a line behind, all the way to their mum stood on the back step. They stand with their hands on their hips and in dresses and cardigans with their hair long and wavy, going up in two-year gaps; their mum on the step is an older version of them. If they walk through the town together you see people turn their heads to watch them. Ronnie looks like his dad. He's the runt of the litter.

Doh move him! my grandad shouts.

Oh Sean!

Oh darling!

Doh move him!

Oh Sean, darling, what have yer done?

I said doh move him, he might've bost his neck.

My grandad's face appears at the window, red and angry-looking. He pulls the sheeting back from the frame, popping rusty nails across the shed like gunshots.

His neck's bost!

A bosted neck!

News of my broken neck is passed back along the line of Robertson girls, and echoes back through my own family, and on down the street, and over Kates Hill and down through Cinderheath, through all of Dudley and on to Tipton and on across England.

I haven't broken my neck, I try to say, but I think maybe I've broken my arse.

If his neck's bost yow cor move him.

My mum starts to pull me up off the dust sheets.

His eyes am open, look yer.

My mum lets me drop back onto the dust sheets and crouches down next to me. Her hair brushes my face.

Sean, can yer hear me, darling? Iss all right, iss all right. Can yer squeeze me hand?

I squeeze her hand and then raise my arms. Ronnie puts his thumbs up and grins before his sisters whisk him away and my grandad mutters, Right as rain, and holds the fist he used to punch Uncle Eric out in front of him like a wounded paw.

My dad arrives from work during the commotion and carries me, on the dust sheets that saved my life, to the kitchen table to lie face down because I can't stand any pressure on my arse. He holds me to his chest, like I weigh nothing at all, that work smell on his open shirt, of soap suds and metal.

There is a debate about whether to go to hospital or not and how we should do it, everyone talking at once. My grandad's right hand is enormous, he can't drive; he holds a bag of frozen peas against it while we talk in the kitchen. He doesn't want to go to hospital, anyway.

I doh need to go to the hospital, sort Sean out, for God's sake.

Yer need that lookin at, my nan says to him. Doh say another word, Jack. Yow've said enough today.

We all go in my dad's car. My grandad sits in the passenger seat with his injured hand in front of him and I lie on my mum and nan across the back seat with my arse in the air. Stella's left to look for her dad.

The radio comes on as the engine starts; Margaret Thatcher's voice fills the car.

Turn her off, will yer, Francis? Her's caused enough trouble for one day.

Stop talking, Jack, my nan says.

Iss her bloody fault, I hear my grandad mutter under his breath.

We sit separately from my nan and grandad at the hospital. Uncle Eric and Stella arrive but they sit away from us too. Uncle Eric is also holding a bag of peas, wrapped in a tea towel, up to his eye. Grandad and Uncle Eric don't look at each other. I see my nan and Stella walk over to the middle of the room and start to talk and my nan puts her hand on Stella's shoulder before my name is called and I get taken through to see the doctor.

I get an X-ray and a lollipop. I have a bruised coccyx and buttocks and hundreds of splinters in my backside.

My mum bursts into tears for no reason when the doctor asks was no one watching me.

I want to say no one could have been watching me because they were all watching my grandad and Uncle Eric have a fight and, anyway, I'm nine years old so don't need watching, but I don't get to say anything. I start to speak but my dad says shush and looks at me and I know better than to say anything. The doctor starts to talk about some cream they have to rub into my backside to get the splinters out and stop infection.

My dad drives me and my mum to my nan and grandad's house. Then he goes back to hospital and gives Uncle Eric and Stella a lift home. Eric's okay; he has a black eye and a few loose teeth. They had to X-ray his eye socket. Then my dad brings my nan and grandad back to the house.

My grandad has broken some bones in his hand and it's bandaged up so it looks about ten times its normal size, like when someone is hurt in a cartoon. I can tell that my nan isn't speaking to my grandad. She stands next to him and stares into space with her lips tight together.

This is what yer needed, I bet, my mum says to my dad as they stand on the back step. Working all hours and now this.

My dad shrugs and smiles at her. Iss all right, he says.
She rubs his back. I bet yome shattered, she says.
I'm tired. I am tired, he says and nods.

This is better, much better, because last night I heard them talking late in the kitchen with the radio playing the election results.

You should be ashamed of yerself, she whispered. I am.
We've got to think about ourselves, my dad said. About us.
To think it, voting Tory.
You'll see. The country's got to change.
Doh say this to nobody else, Francis, will yer?
I ay that saft.
I doh know why yer did it. Yer doh even like politics.
Things am gonna change.
They can change for the worse, yer know, as well as the better.
Just wait and see, my dad says, yow'll see.
I cor see that yome the same person I married. I doh know what's got into yer.

When she said this, my mum walked out of the kitchen to come and turn the hall light off and I had to scramble up the stairs and into bed.

There is the crash of metal somewhere from the works across the allotments.

Dyer think Stella got her broken nail seen to in casualty? my dad says.

Everything is all right.

'Now we have turned inwards
and we seem to be fragmenting
our society and concentrating
on differences between us as
factions pursue their separate aims
relentlessly.'

It was a Friday, the day after the election. We always had fish and chips on a Friday. We must have tried to carry on as normal because I remember that we all ate fish and chips with me face down on the kitchen table. My mum rubbed cream into my wounds and then splashed vinegar on my chips, just the way I liked them.

Well, it ay hurt his appetite, look, my grandad said.

My dad worked with the tweezers. He put the splinters in a jam jar as he plucked them out. I kept the jar for a long time on the windowsill in my bedroom. It looked like a jar of spiders' legs. I had a dream of giant spiders coming over the fence at the back of our house, seeking terrible revenge for the trees, where they once lived, that had been chopped down to make space for the new houses. Every autumn we'd get a plague of spiders. They used to invade my nan and grandad's house too, coming in from the cold off the allotments. My uncle Johnny would sit out on the path and draw the cobwebs with soft pencil in his sketchbook. We lived in the new houses, in Elm Drive, away from Crow Street, and away from Cinderheath and Cromwell Green. There were no elms on Elm Drive, but there were crows on Crow Street. I buried the jar in the garden, in the end. Then, later, when we lost the house, the jar of spiders' legs was gone for ever.

Ronnie comes round to get some peace from his sisters and to borrow some felt pens to get his homework done. We were asked to design our dream house. I'd done mine. It was easy. I went out the back of my nan and grandad's and drew their row, then I turned round and where the allotments are I drew a football pitch. I put the chicken run that Ronnie's dad, Harry, built in their garden, even though they had to get rid of the chickens when the fox attacked and a man from the council came round to tell them off. Ronnie cried for days afterwards; he was the one that found them. He told me there was blood and feathers spattered against the chicken run and that the blood had been bright and shiny on the walls of their little house and then dark and sticky on the ground, thick and nearly black with bits of chicken guts in it. There was a trail of blood and guts out under the fence and into the allotments. Ronnie said if he saw the fox he was going to kill it.

How will yer kill it?

I'll shoot it.

Yow ay gorra gun.

It doh matter, I'll still shoot it. Yow've never sin nothing like it, Sean.

I have.

No, yow ay, doh lie.

I sid me great-granny when her was dead.

Was there blood?

I nodded. I think there was. I day see it, though.

Where?

In a washing-up bowl.

I'll kill the fox, if it comes here again, Sean.

Ronnie crept downstairs for a few nights and waited on

the back steps for the fox. I don't know what he planned
to do. He hasn't got a gun. He hasn't got anything.

In my drawing I kept everything else the same, including
the shed that I fell through. I put in the view of the castle
and all the works and the gantry at Cinderheath, and that
was it. I wish we still lived in Crow Street, at my nan and
grandad's, and not up the road in our new house, but I
don't say anything.

Crow Street runs down and off Kates Hill like the way
water does in a storm. At the bottom you can turn into
Cromwell Green Road or head straight over the main road
for Cinderheath. You used to be able to turn left to go up
into the town, into Dudley, but there's a wall there now and
the roar of traffic on the new bypass behind that. You have
to walk the long way round these days, although I don't
suppose anyone bothers. In those days, if you looked over
the fence you'd see all the factories spread out beyond the
allotments and to the left, the castle on the hill; hard and
bone-coloured in the sun, grey in the wet, staring out over
us. The quickest way to Cinderheath was along one of the
winding paths through the allotments. That was the way my
grandad went to and from work, loads of the other men too.

The Robertsons lived in the end house of the row, so
they had an extra bedroom, but it was still too crowded
with the five girls and Ronnie. Next came my nan and
grandad's. In the other end house Jermaine, another friend
from school, lived with his mum and sister, and sometimes
his stepdad. In between was Mr and Mrs Blower's house.
They were old, and to me then seemed as ancient as the
pharaohs. Their daughter, Geraldine, who was nearly the
same age as my nan, used to bring their dinners on a plate

every day and shout 'Meals on Wheels' down the entry. The Blowers had a tortoise called Albert. In the summer, he'd walk up and down the back garden and Geraldine would bring him a bit of lettuce for his meals on wheels. Ronnie would come round and we'd feed him the lettuce through the fence. Jermaine painted his shell once, with two little pots of paint you get for model planes: airforce blue and steel grey. The Blowers didn't like it and Geraldine and Jermaine's mum had a row across the fence.

Letting that child run wild while yome up to yer tricks up theer.

Woss that meant to mean, yer jealous, dried-up old bitch?

Albert didn't seem to mind the paint. Mr Blower told us that Albert used to have a wife called Victoria but she'd long gone. Albert was as old as the Boer War. He'd moved with the Blowers from their old house in the town to this house when it was new, in 1936. My grandad told me that he thought Albert used to die and rise again most years, that he didn't make it through the winter in his shoebox in the airing cupboard and that if you looked carefully the tortoise had a different shell each spring.

The houses continued in fours all the way back up the hill. Paul lived with his mum, brother and sister about halfway up and me, Ronnie and Jermaine would knock for him on the way to school. The school was at the top of the hill.

Elm Drive is right down the other end of Cromwell Green Road. Our house was brand-new then. The windows of my room looked out over our back fence at the space where the old dairy had been, which was laid out as plots for more new houses. My grandad said that when he was a boy he used to walk all the way to the cow sheds that had been here to stroke the cows' fat, wet noses; beyond that had been the trees: ash, sycamore, elm, and a lane that used to run through a farm and into Oakham.

I liked the smell of the new carpets at first, lying flat in the empty rooms, looking at the clean white walls, but the smell faded and the truth was that I didn't like our house even then. It was too far from Crow Street, too quiet, too on the edge of things. And there were no other children. I worried I'd be made to leave school and go somewhere closer to Elm Drive. They were building a new school up the road to serve the new houses. Things were changing. I wanted to see the castle and the factories and live near to Ronnie and the others and to hear Charlie Clancey's cart come clip-clopping past on Fridays, with his shout of Ragabooen, Ragabooen, becoming louder and louder as he came down Cromwell Green Road and then drifting away as he went up Crow Street. He'd often stop the cart and have a chat with Ronnie's dad. Sometimes he'd let us pat the horse. He had a few that lived in the field behind his yard but on Fridays it was always the same tall brown one, breathing hard before starting up the hill. The horse was skinny like Charlie. Ronnie would reach up to stroke his ear but I would hold back, wary, looking at the horse's ribs and angry eyes. It would shit on the road in front of the houses and sometimes Charlie would jump down and scrape it up into a metal bucket and sometimes it would just stay there in the road.

Disgusting, my nan said. He shouldn't be allowed in this day and age.

I need to set me a lad on soon. I need a mate, Charlie would always say. He used to touch his back gingerly if he'd jumped down from the cart. One o yow two can start coming wi me, eh?

Neither me nor Ronnie mentioned it to the other because we both wanted to do it. One night, sat on the back step, Ronnie said, We could do every other wik, me one Friday, yow the next, split the money.

What?

Wi Charlie. We could do one wik on, one wik off. Share it.

Or we could see if he'd tek us both. Split the money, course.

I remember being glad we'd talked about it but the chance never came. I don't know if Charlie had ever been serious or not.

For ages I thought Ragabooen was the horse's name before I realized. The horse was called Paul Newman.

There is a story of the black wagon they used to pull round Kates Hill during the cholera epidemic back in Victorian times. A man left one of the old pubs, the Sailor's Return maybe, after having a few too many late at night, when they were collecting the dead. The day's bodies were left at the side of the road for collection. The man left the pub as the wagon was coming past. Startled, the horse, driver and driver's mate turned towards him. They were skeletons; all three. The driver's mate pointed his bony finger at the man. The next day he told the story; the day after that he died. In the pub I tell people that you can sometimes see them, on moonlit nights, coming down St John's Road, their ghost cart piled high with bodies. You can hear the slow plod of a horse's hooves and the creak of the cart's wheels through the winding maze of the flats. They used to dump the bodies in a pit behind the churchyard; too many to bury. That part is true.

I stayed quiet about not liking our new house. It was important to my dad. The house he grew up in had gone, blown to pieces when they joined the quarries together. I wonder now if that was why owning a house became such a big deal for him, like that would protect him, an Englishman's home and all that.

Ronnie's going crazy with the felt tips. He's already got his own motor racing track, a swimming pool, some robot servants, a Wimpy restaurant instead of a kitchen, and a helipad. While they pluck my arse everyone starts chipping in with ideas for the dream house.

What about a beauty parlour, Ron? my nan says.

What? he says.

Yer know, for yer hair and legs and that.

I doh need a beauty parlour. He pushes his glasses right back on his nose and sniffs. My mum starts to laugh.

Yer sisters might like one, though, Ronnie, and yer mom.

They ay gonna live theer. Ronnie grins as he says this. He has to share a room with two of his sisters.

How about when they visit?

He weighs this up.

How about a rodeo, Ronnie? Yer know, like we watched on that cowboy film last wik, my grandad says.

Arr, okay.

My nan glares at my grandad. She's still not speaking to him.

When Ronnie's added the beauty parlour, rodeo, snooker room and the disco glitterballs that my mum suggests, he's done.

Hope yome feelin better soon, he says to me, and taps me on the shoulder like he's seen his dad do when he's out in the street talking about cars.

Thanks, I say.

I know what's coming next.

Have you done yours, Sean? my mum says.

Yeah.

What's it like?

Oh, I copied one of the houses off that leaflet dad brought back the other day.

Yer should've asked yer uncle Johnny to have a look at it.

My uncle Johnny did art at college for a while. Then he had a row with my grandad about turning some rent up every now and again so now he works in a place that makes steel window frames, a factory like all the others. It's funny because now that he goes to work and gives my nan a bundle of notes on a Friday night my grandad keeps nagging about when he's going to go back to college. He's always asking to have a look at his sketchbook and telling him how good his work is, when before he'd always ask him what he was wasting his time for and if he was painting a flower why couldn't he make it look like a flower. Johnny told me he might go back to college sometime soon or that he might go and live in France. He wants to be an artist like Vincent van Gogh. Van Gogh's his favourite artist; mine too. I can't draw or anything like that. I'm rubbish at it. I don't want Johnny to see how bad I am.

I shout out and pretend that my arse is hurting. It isn't. Well, no more than it was before, but I don't want to have to talk about the dream house any more. The leaflet my dad brought home was from the estate agent's with houses in Kingswinford and Wall Heath, places like that, almost the countryside. I don't want to move again. I don't know why I said I drew one of them. They're miles away. I would definitely have to change school.

Maybe we'll live in a house like that one day. My mum smiles.

My mum's not even that bothered herself. I heard them talking. I wasn't meant to have.

I'll live anywhere, Francis, really. I doh care. As long as we'm all together. To keep wanting more's no good. It just goes on and on.

Yome just saying that. If I took yer there and said here, we can live here in this house, yow'd love it.

Maybe.

Or dyer wanna stop in places like the flat or yer mum and dad's all yer life?

Well, iss better here, obviously.

Course it is, and there's places that am better again. We'll keep gooin and gooin. Why not? Why shouldn't we? The people that live there am no better than we am, they got more money, thass all.

I know that, my mum says. I ay the one that needs convincing of that.

They talk about this a lot: houses and where we might end up living. My grandad says our house is already more trouble than it's worth. I wasn't meant to have heard him. He said it under his breath. He said it when my mum was making some curtains with my nan. I agree with him.

When we got that work given back at school, the comment on mine said, Very unimaginative and not up to your usual high standards. Ronnie got called out the front of the class and his work got put on the wall, a mess of felt pen and my family's ambitions.

'And I would just like to remember some words of Saint Francis of Assisi which I think are really just particularly apt at the moment. Where there is discord, may we bring harmony. Where there is error, may we bring truth. Where there is doubt, may we bring faith. And where there is despair, may we bring hope.'

Where there is discord, she said, on the glowing television set while everyone ate their fish and chips. Where there is doubt. There was a picture of Saint Francis up above the telly, next to the family photos. My nan ended up taking the picture down out of shame, so Saint Francis didn't have to look. You could see the outline of the frame for years afterwards. Where there is despair.

We used to visit Saint Francis's Church on the other side of the town to see the stained-glass windows of Duncan Edwards. There's a window with him in his England shirt and another in his Man United one. I took my own boy, Joshua, to show him. I remember how proud we were that the world's best footballer had come from Dudley, like it said something important about all of us. I liked the way the sun came through the windows and the gentle red light that the United shirt cast on the floor. *Though there are many numbers*, the window said, *yet there is one · body*. We knew that it meant you had to stick together. We used to tell each other how, even though he had such terrible injuries, he'd lived for fifteen days after the crash and that the doctors had never seen anyone as strong and brave. That was what you had to be like if you were from Dudley. I remember thinking that if I had died and gone to heaven, I'd have got to play football with him, probably.

My ambition then was to get the older boys to let me play in the game on the big playground at school.

I thought Saint Francis was from Dudley too, for a time, because it was my dad's name maybe, or because of these visits to the church. I thought that Assisi was another area like, say, the Wren's Nest or Sledmere or Kates Hill. I used to imagine him talking to Jennie Lee, the budgie; or to Caesar the Alsatian that padded up and down behind the gate at the Ash Tree and used to wait for me and Ronnie to come and run sticks along the railings to send him into a child-eating frenzy; or to the giraffes at the zoo. It was a while later, when I chose to do a school project on Saint Francis, to the delight of my nan and Sister Marie Antoinette, that I found out that Assisi was in Italy. We had to do all the work in a scrapbook, with pictures and cut-outs and different writing exercises. I kept my projects for years afterwards: The Life of Saint Francis, Dudley Zoo, Fossils of Dudley, A History of the Ashes Series, The Gunpowder Plot. Most of the other kids used to pick cars or horses, that kind of thing, so usually I'd win a prize, although one year Paul and Jermaine did a complete cartoon strip of that match that finished Man United 3–West Brom 5, so they won.

I remember reading their comic open-mouthed it was so good, almost as good as Johnny's paintings, like I was turning the pages of a holy book. I can see one page even now, with GOAL! written in thick black lettering and Laurie Cunningham bursting from the letter O like he would run off the page and across your lap, Man United defenders lying at his feet.

I wonder what happens to these relics; imagine civilizations piecing together shards of the stained-glass windows and scraps of Jermaine's illustrated manuscript ages in the future. One of Jermaine's sons used to come into the pub for a while. I told him his dad was a good artist once and he just laughed and said, Piss artist. Jermaine moved to Birmingham and I stopped speaking to Paul Hill after he put me in hospital. But all this came years later. Me and Little Ronnie tried to do a comic strip of Alex Higgins knocking in a century break, but neither of us could draw that well and Alex Higgins looked like a monkey holding a long banana.

My uncle Johnny arrives home as we eat fish and chips. I want to be like him. He had to do overtime tonight to make up for not doing it earlier in the week because he's been going out and working on the election. He even made a poster that some people have put up in their windows. It says DUDLEY EAST, VOTE LABOUR, VOTE DR JOHN GILBERT, *in red letters. Jim Bayliss, who's in the Labour Party, and who Johnny's been delivering leaflets for, got them printed up. The original, which Johnny painted on cardboard on the kitchen table on a Sunday morning a few weeks ago, is on the wall of his bedroom next to Peter Shilton and David Bowie and* Wheatfield with Crows. *My grandad put the poster up in the front-room window. I've seen them up in people's houses on the way to school. I tried to put one up at our house. My mum told me to take it down.*
Why?
Take it down, Sean.
Why can't we put it up, like at nan and grandad's?
Nobody'll see it, Sean. There's no point.
Course they'll see it. Everybody in the street'll see it.
It's not a good idea, darling.

Why not?

Sean, I said no.

Johnny slumps down in a chair and rubs his face; his eyes look tired. All the posters have to come down now. My dad cracks open a bottle of Newcastle Brown for him; they like to drink that together. My nan has kept a plate of chips warm. Johnny has a load of badges on his jacket. He passes them on to me: Steel Pulse, Steve Biko, CND. I pin them to my school parka.

They tell Johnny the story of how I fell out the window to cheer him up and it's good to see how my mum and dad turn it into a funny story, even though at the time they thought I might be dead. He starts to laugh and comes over and ruffles my hair.

What happened to your hand, Dad? Johnny says.

No one says anything.

I'll tell yer later, my mum says to Johnny.

We turn Margaret Thatcher off.

Her woh last five minutes, any road. Johnny says, doing a voice like my grandad's.

My grandad says not to be so sure. My mum agrees. My dad doesn't say anything.

I'm happy because they decide that I've done enough moving around for today and I get to spend the night at my nan and grandad's house. I love staying here, especially when my grandad is off work. He's just finished a week of nights. His voice is tired and cracked and I think maybe that was why he lost his temper with my uncle Eric and why Margaret Thatcher has got to him so much.

My dad has to go back to work because a machine breaks down and only he can fix it. He's got an important job, maintenance at Coopers Steel Stampings, making sure

the machines that cut the metal work properly. My mum
sleeps in the single bed next to mine in the room I fell out
of. I dream of falling and she holds my hand.

Next morning, my mum eats toast at the kitchen table.
She has some shopping to do and wants to get out before
it gets too busy, especially now it's clear that I'm fine. I
know that my dad is going to meet her when he's finished
at work and they are going to look at one of those houses
in Kingswinford or somewhere else miles away.

Am yer sure you didn't bang anything else, sweetheart?
my mum asks and holds my shoulders so she can look into
my eyes. Yer didn't bang yer head?

Just me bum.

You haven't got a headache or nothing?

Just arse-ache!

Don't say arse, Sean.

What else should I call it?

Yer bottom or yer bum. Yer behind.

Just bum-ache, then.

Yer know what you'll look like when the bruise comes
out?

What?

A baboon. A baboon with a bright blue bum!

She does a little dance like a monkey that makes me
laugh and kisses me again on the top of my head before
she leaves for the shops.

My grandad sits in his usual seat at the table, dipping
toast into a fried egg with his good hand. My nan stands
at the window, singing bits of songs and drinking tea.

What's Picasso doin today, lyin in bed? My grandad nods
upstairs towards my uncle Johnny's bedroom.

He wants a rest, my nan says.

He's a good lad, my grandad says after a while.

My nan doesn't say anything. She's still angry with my grandad about fighting Uncle Eric. I think she's angry with him about making Johnny leave college as well, but she keeps quiet about that.

My grandad has taken the big bandages off his hand even though the hospital said he was meant to leave them on for a week and then go back. He has wrapped one bandage around his hand himself. I can see the tips of his fingers, like sausages, where he holds his knife.

My nan sings quietly and wipes the draining board with a cloth.

Mind you, we could do wi some help tekkin that shed down, couldn't we, mate? My grandad winks at me. Yow've onny done half a job, look. We'll have to finish it off today.

Doh listen to him, Sean. My nan kisses me on the top of my head in the same way as my mum does. Wim lucky yome okay. Lucky we ay all still dahn the hospital. We should be thankful for what we've got. Then she looks at my grandad. I doh know how you think yer can mek light of it now, when it was all yower fault.

We know whose fault it was.

I'm not sure if he means Margaret Thatcher or my uncle Eric.

There is a knock at the front door. I follow my nan to see who it can be. No one usually comes to the front door; they either come up the entry or along the path from the allotments.

Oh my God, my nan says and puts her hand up to her mouth when she opens the door. There's a policeman on the step, filling the doorway, and another one standing out on the pavement.

Jack, iss the police, she says.

Well, they better come in then.

My grandad has followed us and shows the policemen into the front room to sit down even before the first policeman says, We'd like to have a word with you, Mr Marsh.

No one ever goes in the front room, except on Sundays or Christmas or maybe bank holidays when everyone comes round. The best cups are in there and my great-granny's sideboard and the good armchairs from Cooks and the telephone. On special occasions my grandad and Uncle Eric phone Australia to speak to their brother, my uncle Freddie, who lives in a place called Wollongong.

My grandad offers the police the good chairs and says, I spose I can guess what this is about, before closing the door behind them.

No, they never spoke to each other ever again, my grandad and Uncle Eric, though they'd often see each other in town or at the club and even at the caravans on holiday during a couple of summers; not one word.

I don't know how the police came to visit that morning. I can't really believe Eric called them. Nothing came of it. Well, nothing except a sense of unease and the idea that one morning there might be another knock on the door.

The police to our door? I remember my nan saying. Three-quarters of an hour they was here. We've never had the police to our door.

She kept shaking her head and saying it over and over. They were to come again, later.

'My policies are based not on
some economics theory, but
on things I and millions like
me were brought up with:
an honest day's work for an
honest day's pay; live within
your means; put by a nest egg
for a rainy day; pay your bills
on time; support the police.'

My grandad is a strong man. He takes the shed down in about five minutes, even with his bad hand. He's pretending there's nothing wrong with it; maybe because my nan is watching, shaking her head, muttering about the police. He doesn't look it. I mean, he doesn't look like the strong men in my comics: Desperate Dan, Johnny Cougar, Hot Shot Hamish. He's skinny, like a whippet. When he takes his shirt off, when he takes me swimming or at the caravan on holiday, you can see his ribs but also hard knots of muscle up and down his body from all the lifting and twisting he does at work, and the blurry blue tattoos up his arms. He lifts a whole wall of the shed out of its foundation with a cigarette hanging out of his mouth.

He hasn't said anything since the police left apart from when my nan said, Well, is anything more gonna come of it?

He said, Doh be so saft. Bloody fool him. Yow'd think the police would have better things to do than come drinking tay in our front room on a Saturday morning.

All the stuff that had been in the shed is laid out on the lawn, like there's been an earthquake or a flood. Two bikes, an old rusted pink one with a basket that had been my mum's and an ancient racer that had been my uncle Eric's that I imagine myself riding in a few years' time

34

if we can clean it up; a few tennis rackets with broken strings; deckchairs and a windbreak; Johnny's easel that was broken when he fought the skinheads; a hosepipe; a tool box; a cricket bat; a few golf balls; tennis balls; and the pile of dust sheets that saved my life. There's an old, battered, rusty box with a lock on it as well.

What's in that box? my nan says.

My grandad shrugs and pretends not to know.

There's a gun in the box that I'm not meant to know about. I don't say anything, either. I could've told Ronnie about it, I suppose. He could've used it to shoot the fox.

My grandad used to talk with a cigarette in his mouth and the cigarette would move up and down as he spoke. I liked it when we sat outside in the summer or at the caravans on holiday and you'd see the orange glow of the cigarette moving up and down as it got dark. Years later, when I had my own family, on holiday in Majorca, I walked Josh and Lily back to our cabin during a power cut. In a clump of undergrowth outside the door was a glow-worm. Lily stood transfixed, while I held Josh, a toddler then, to stop him making a grab for it. I found myself looking not at a glow-worm, but at the wobble of a lit cigarette back here in the Black Country dark.

I think my grandad was the only one who had any idea what was coming.

We drive to the tip and listen to a tape of Nat King Cole. My grandad keeps his bandaged hand fixed on the steering wheel. The car is a silvery blue Maxi that he bought from Harry Robertson. Little Ronnie's dad sells cars in the street after he's done them up. My grandad puts the

back seat down to fit in the bits of the shed that he hasn't
saved for a bonfire and a few other bags of rubbish that
he's been waiting to get rid of. I get to sit in the front,
which usually is a big deal, but we can't solve the problem
of my sitting down. My nan gives me a cushion but it's
no use, the minute we start moving and my arse makes
contact with the seat, I'm in agony. We have to pull up in
the bus stop on Cromwell Green Road for my grandad
to arrange my great-granny's mattress in the back. I can
smell her on there. It doesn't bother me, though. I've seen
her dead, with her arms pulled up into her chest and her
mouth a little way open. My mum had shooed me out of
the room when I followed her. My great-granny was laid
out like the mummies at the museum that I'd seen on telly.
She was born in 1887 or 1888, no one was sure.
  We could check. They have records.
  Not for the likes o we, my mum said.
  I have no idea what she meant.

A few years ago, though, I did check and she was right.
There is no sign of us in any of the parish records, at
the Catholic churches round and about; at the Church
of England, Top or Bottom Churches, at Saint John's on
Kates Hill; at the Methodist, the Baptist. Our family moved
back and forth between churches over the years. We knew
we were here by then, though, drawn to the glow of the
town from the dark fields round about, or from Wales
even; bringing our anvils and bits of iron with us. There
was an afternoon before my great-granny died when she
started talking in a language that no one could understand.
  Is it Welsh? my grandad had said.
  Nonsense, my nan said and shook her head.

My grandad might have been making some sort of joke but the thought stayed with me, that she had gone back to some earlier time and was using language she'd heard her own father or grandfather use. I picture a man looking back to his mountains, following the road to where there was work.

Nobody wrote us down for a long time, not until we mattered, I suppose.

My grandad said he knew where some of his family came from: out near Clent, where they'd had little furnaces in the woods; before the country was called England, when it was called Mercia. Some of us were here even then.

There are seagulls at the tip. Hungry and angry, they circle the pit, where you throw things and they call to each other and sometimes flap down to peck and tear at bags and pieces of sacking. I wonder if they miss the sea. I have only ever been to the tip with my dad before and he makes me stay in the car. There are men in the pit, picking things out like the seagulls.

What they doing, Grandad?

Looking for treasure, he says.

I stand by the open boot and pass things to him.

Charlie Clancey comes over to talk to us. He's at the tip looking for rag and bone. I look for Paul Newman, but Charlie's only got his van today. Charlie pats me on the head and passes me a few coins from his pocket. One of the coins is American, ten cents, a dime.

I kept that coin for years afterwards, for luck. Then I threw it in the canal like Mohammad Ali with his gold medal. *Ain't No Viet Cong ever call me Nigger.* Johnny had that on a poster on his bedroom wall. My grandad used to call Ali Cassius Clay to wind Johnny up.

Charlie smells like the pit. He shakes hands with my grandad, who has to use his left hand. Charlie nods at the bandage and asks him what he's done and my grandad doesn't answer, asks him to help with the mattress instead. We are related to Charlie, somehow, distantly, like he's our cousin's cousin's cousin. We are related to everyone somehow. I see Charlie have a look at the mattress as we pull it out of the car, press his bony hand to it, working out whether it's rag or bone. He shakes his head and they fling it together over the edge.

No sign of Tommy yet, then, Charlie?

No, yer know what he's like.

Charlie's brother is missing. He's a bit like a tramp, comes and goes as he pleases. He looks exactly like Charlie, tall and thin, with skin stretched across knobbly bones, except a bit more beaten up; Tommy wears a blue checked cap and Charlie wears a brown hat with a feather in it. That's a good way to tell them apart.

I've spoken to Tommy a couple of times at the Off Sales hatch at the Freebodies Tavern. Both times Tommy was drunk, sitting on the edge of the pavement, waiting for a customer to come to the bar so they might buy him more beer.

One time I was with my dad when Tommy stepped towards us. My dad said, Yow got a problem, mate? Tommy stepped back and muttered, No problem, no problem, our kid, and looked at me. I doubt he could have fought my dad, but you weren't meant to fight your own family anyway, even distant family, whatever my grandad had done to my uncle Eric.

That was Tommy, I said to my dad as we walked to the car.

I doh care who it was, he said.

The other time I saw him was in exactly the same place but this time I was with my grandad, who gave him some cigarettes.

Ta, Jackie. Ta, me mon, Tommy said to my grandad and patted him on the arm. His hands were all dirty and looked like they'd been bleeding.

Tek it easy, Tommy, for Christ's sake. Goo um now, eh? My grandad had pointed somewhere down the hill, probably towards Charlie's yard. Doh tell yer nan about Tommy, he said to me.

Charlie looks out over the tip.

Yer know what he's like. With the summer coming I probly woh see him till October now, not till the weather gets bad. Yer know what he's like. I heared he'd gone down Stourport again. I had a mate who said he'd sin him, Easter. He'll turn up. Or there'll be a knock at the door one day. Any road.

Charlie shrugs, slaps his hands together again and holds one out for my grandad to shake, his left to make it easier. I get ready to shake hands as well but he just pats me on the shoulder.

Without the mattress, the car shakes me about, rattling my bones as we drive over the gravel road out of the tip. My grandad sings along to Nat King Cole like he does on Sunday nights when he's had a few drinks and I wriggle around and try not to get too shaken up.

Up in Dudley we go to a few shops. My grandad has instructions from my nan about some things he has to get and we have to buy a bag of nails from a man on the market to help grandad build a new shed. He stops and says hello to everyone and because I've been patient and because my arse feels like it's on fire he takes me up to the toy shop and lets me buy a Star Wars figure. I choose a Jawa. The Jawas travel around looking for scrap metal in their sandcrawlers. I think about Charlie Clancey and his rag and bone.

My grandad looks at me and says, Am yer sure yer want that little un? He looks at the hooded figure in the packet but it's my choice and I say, Yes.

The brewery is at work on the top of the hill and the wind is blowing down into the town, so you can smell the hops. My mum tells stories about when they all used to go hop-picking, out past Worcester, in the summers when she was a little girl, before Johnny was born. I like the brewery smell, drink it in. I enjoy it when you get to see through the doors of the pubs in the town or when my dad or grandad take me to the Off Sales hatch at the Lion or the Freebodies and you see through into the bar and hear the clack of the dominoes or see the men standing up or sitting and staring into space; like they are thinking really hard about something, or reading the paper, or talking quietly about serious things or telling jokes but not laughing as they tell them; the way you are meant to, when you're a man. Usually, you can't see anything. All the pubs have glass that you can't see through. It makes you want to look more. You can see the men now, though, waiting for the pubs to open. They step from foot to foot and their shadows tremble out into the street. At opening time we cross the road where Stafford Street meets the High Street and I see Ronnie's mum at the door of the pub called the Shrewsbury Arms, which everyone calls the Cow Shed. She's talking to a man wearing a suit. It might be one of her brothers, one

*of the Woodhouses, going to court, except it's Saturday,
so there's no court.*

*They'm never out of court, I'd heard my nan say. I begin
to wave but my grandad pulls on my arm to get me across
the road.*

*Iss Ronnie's mum, Grandad. I point. She must've gone
in the pub. We should say hello.*

*Doh bother her now, he says, which I think is strange
because usually he likes leaning on the fence, between the
shed and the gate to the allotments and talking to her as
she collects the washing in. Sometimes my nan tells him
off for pestering her.*

There were hundreds of pubs in Dudley. My grandad told
me about them all. The Albion and the Gypsies' Tent and
the Smiling Man. Further afield: the Hangsman's Tree, the
Swan with Two Necks, the Pig on the Wall. You could tell a
whole history of a place from its pub names. The first thing
I did when I took our pub on was go back to the original
name: the Crow Cawing. It's an old place. Roundheads
drank in a tavern here, there was badger baiting in the
hollow out the back that is now the chemist's uneven car
park; they used to read the Chartist newspaper out loud to
crowds of men in the front bar. In the rebellion, in 1842,
the people made tiswases in the nail yard that was next
door, three nails hammered together to throw under the
army horses' hooves. When they got taken to Worcester
Assizes the nailers would be asked for their plea and they'd
say, I plead starvation, before being led off to the cart that
would take them to the boat for Australia.

That Saturday morning we stopped on the corner at the
bottom of the High Street. There'd once been a pub here

called The Welch Go By, meaning the Welsh. They must have driven their sheep this way to the markets, maybe my great-granny had come with them. Round the corner, where the bus station was, was where both my nan and grandad grew up. They got married at the end of the war. This was after all the houses had been knocked down and everyone moved out to the estates. We stopped outside the television shop. People would stand there to check the cricket scores or wait for the football results on Saturday teatimes. That day, all the screens in the window had Margaret Thatcher's face on them.

All the screens have Margaret Thatcher's face on them. There are hundreds of them. She's giving a speech. Hundreds of screens, faces; she looks down at us. It's like she's telling us all off, but we can't hear her.

Oh, bloody hell, my grandad says, like he's forgotten all about something and remembered it suddenly. He unravels the bandage from his hand and then wraps it back up again.

From then on she was always there, a picture on the television hundreds of times over; sometimes only her voice, nagging away across the allotments and gardens and factories; the meanness of it, her voice, working away at you like rust.

'Now, with increasing frequency, neighbour strikes against neighbour, and common humanity is being displaced by action against the most vulnerable of our people in the battle for pay and power.'

All the standing up after my injury makes my legs strong. I can feel them grow, feel the muscles harden. For a few days I drop my trousers at the start of playtime to show everyone the bruise. The first time I do it, it's for Ronnie, who's already seen it on his back step, and Paul and Jermaine, but the next couple of days the whole class crowds round, girls too, which makes me feel a bit funny, especially when Michelle Campbell shouts, *I can see his willy*, when she can't because I've got my hands over it. She's got a big mouth. I try to be angry with Michelle, but the feeling I get is different from being angry with her. I stand behind her in the classroom and look at the bobbles in her hair and her shiny ear-rings, even though it's against the rules to wear them. I wait for her to turn around and laugh.

Everyone gets bored of my arse as the bruising fades. I have to stop dropping my trousers anyway because Miss Wright gets suspicious of what's happening in the cloakroom and starts to stand at the door at break-times.

Her wants to see yer willy, Michelle whispers.

Someone has been to the boys' toilets two days running and gone all over the floor. Miss Wright gives us a long speech about how it's dirty and how whoever did it might need some help so we have to come straight out and own up or tell her who it was if we knew.

Nobody's telling tales. Nobody knows who it is, anyway. Jermaine turns to me and says, Is it yow?

I try to do a face like my grandad when he thinks my uncle Johnny has said something stupid. I am worried, though. I think Michelle might go and tell Miss Wright it's me for a laugh. My mum has written a note to allow me to stand up in lessons after my accident. Miss Wright might think the two things are connected.

The toilet stayed a mystery for a long time. We'd go in there at break and there'd be a long brown turd on the tiled floor waiting for us. Miss Wright went frantic. We had an assembly about it. The teachers kept saying that the person doing it might need help, but I remember realizing that what they really meant was whoever was doing it was in big trouble. Then one morning, the word SHIT was smeared on the toilet wall. The S and H were thick and big and the I and T were smeared greasily across the tiles, falling away, like the writer had run out of shit and energy at the same time, as if the weight of it had pulled them earthwards. There was a handprint on one of the white china sinks. Michelle told us we were going to get our fingerprints taken so they could find who it was.

They used their poo as a pen, Jermaine kept saying and couldn't stop laughing. That was it, then; the teachers locked the toilets. If we wanted to go a teacher had to go in there with us.

It was Jermaine, and no one gave him any help. Not long afterwards he got shunted to his real dad's family in Birmingham and we never saw him at school again. Miss Wright made sure we all knew it was Jermaine. He got into trouble, spells in secure units and, later, Winson

Green. He came in the pub not long after I first took it on. He'd have been twenty-eight, twenty-nine then, visiting his mum who had gone back to live with her own mum and dad on the Rosland estate somewhere. He wasn't in a good way, probably shouldn't have been drinking with his medication. His face was scratched with tattoos, like a Maori warrior. I asked him if he still did any drawing or anything like that and he just looked at me. It was a stupid question, I know; his left hand shaking and the other holding his pint. He showed me photos of his kids. He didn't see them much; three of them, different mothers, different areas, round and about. He hanged himself on Christmas Day a few years ago in a flat above a row of shops in Darlaston. I'd have gone to the funeral if I'd found out in time.

When that lad said piss artist when I told him about his dad's drawing I swear it took me all my strength not to get the bat from under the bar and give him the hiding he was asking for.

The shit on the toilet floor at school makes me think of that spring of the hunger strikers, although they came a couple of years later, when things started to get really bad. I remember some terrible arguments between Johnny and my grandad.

It's stopping up, Johnny said, from the landing.

An I've tode yer iss comin down.

It ay.

This is my house an I'll decide what gos up on the walls. Iss comin down.

Johnny had a poster of Bobby Sands up on his wall. I knew that Bobby Sands was in prison and on hunger strike. The idea of having nothing to eat or drink on purpose was so extraordinary to me that I'd watch every news bulletin and try to snatch glimpses of the hunger strikers in my grandad's paper. When Johnny told me about the dirty protests, of the prisoners going on the blanket, naked, shitting and pissing in their cells, it created a kind of ghoulish glamour that appealed to an eleven-year-old boy, and made some foreboding echo of Jermaine's behaviour in my head.

My mum told me that I couldn't watch the news, that she wasn't watching it either because it was too horrible, but I'd catch her with my nan, their hands to their mouths, watching updates about the state of the prisoners' health and Margaret Thatcher's voice saying she would let them die before she gave in.

What's the point, though? I asked Johnny.

Well, the point is, they'm taking a stand, they'm shaming Margaret Thatcher.

Her's got no shame, that's what Grandad says.

Well, I agree with him, for once, but the point is her will be shamed because either they'll die, and her'll have let them die, or her'll have to back down.

And what is it they want to happen?

They want to be not treated like criminals. They'm political prisoners. That means they're in prison because of what they think not because of what they've done.

Did Margaret Thatcher put them in prison?

Well, yeah, she wants them in prison, yeah.

For what they think?

Yeah.

What about you?

What?

Will you get in prison for what you think?

47

I expected him to say, No, doh be so saft, like my grandad would, or, No, that kind of thing doesn't happen here. Instead, he said, Well, if I was, I'd be proud.

Johnny was my hero for a long time. We'd all lived together when I was a baby and then again during the long, hot summer of my sixth birthday when Johnny was seventeen, while our house got finished, after we'd moved out of the flats. He'd done a year's work after leaving school, sweeping up in a factory, and had finally persuaded my grandad he should go to college, so he packed in his job and had August at home watching England and the West Indies play cricket on the telly and filling a paddling pool for me and Ronnie and his sisters to jump in and out of in the back garden. He'd sit and supervise us in my grandad's deckchair, reading the *Daily Mirror* with his shirt off, wearing a floppy hat like Clive Lloyd, the West Indies captain; tensing the muscles he'd grown from sweeping bits of metal across a factory floor; sketching, and drinking the odd bottle of Newcastle Brown Ale. Afternoons, we emptied the pool and he'd wander across the allotments to water the dying plants. There was a hosepipe ban and the men would give him silver coins for the water. Sometimes he'd get Natalie Robertson to walk down one of the paths with him. I saw them kissing once, leaned against some fence panelling that faced towards West Brom. She went off with someone else when the weather broke. There was a pile of drawings he'd done of her naked in his sock drawer. At night he'd play David Bowie LPs over and over on the record player in his room until my mum or dad would bang on the wall to get him to turn the volume down.

What do they think, Bobby Sands and that?

Well, they want Ireland, all of Ireland, to be a separate country. They don't want the English soldiers to be there or for Ireland to be divided into two, like it is now with a British bit and an Irish bit. It's called a war of liberation. Liberation means freedom. They'm trying to free theerselves.

Why doh they fight the soldiers to make em leave?

They do, but the soldiers am very powerful, they've got the whole British army, and the rebels ay got much, so they have to work out different ways to fight them. It's what always happens when powerful countries invade less powerful ones.

Like bullying.

Exactly, it's exactly like bullying. It's a way of fighting against the bullies even if you cor beat em in a fight.

I remember thinking even then that the easiest way to fight a bully was to bully them right back, to fight fire with fire, like Johnny had with the skinheads. He told me that when they broke his easel he went for them, even though there was twenty, thirty of them. He kung-fued one of them into the canal. He told me he thought he might have killed one of them. I said I hoped he had. Now, I realize that could not be true, not in the way he told it, anyway, but I still wish he had. There must have been some yearning in the way he told me about it, with his black eye and his cracked ribs, some dream of fighting back, fighting fire with fire, that took hold of me.

I knew Margaret Thatcher would let Bobby Sands die, it was obvious. He wasn't hurting her.

The poster didn't come down. It stayed up in Johnny's room. He's probably still got it somewhere; he keeps everything. He moved it from the door as some sort of compromise. He put him up next to Peter Shilton. Johnny played in goal for a while at Cinderheath. After Shilton made that mistake to let the Wolves win the cup he liked him even more.

My grandad stayed angry. On the night of the argument he got up halfway through his chips and walked outside. While we finished eating I could see that he'd gone over the road and was standing next to one of Harry Robertson's old bangers, pretending to have a cigarette in the spring air, checking you couldn't see the Bobby Sands poster from the street.

Thass all we need, I heard him saying to my nan later, a bloody brick though the winder.

'On this the government will not compromise. It is not prepared, through the granting of political status, to legitimize criminal acts undertaken in pursuit of political ends.'

At break-times me, Ronnie, Jermaine and Paul stand on the edge of the big boys' football game behind the goal. If the ball comes onto our playground we chase it and fetch it for the bigger boys and try to pass it back to them, with the inside of our foot to show what good players we are and that they should ask us to come and play.

Loads of kids are already on holiday. The car works and some of the factories connected to them all shut down for two weeks so some of the school go off on holiday before the six weeks' break. It's good because we can't really do proper lessons, we do project work and find things out for ourselves. It's the cricket season. A set of stumps is painted on the wall and we borrow a milk crate for the other end, but football has carried on right into July and the older boys are always a few short.

Rodney James calls us on from behind the goal to play for his team against Michael Campbell's. Rodney's a good footballer but Michael's the cock of the school, so his team usually wins. Michael is Michelle's older brother. If I say anything to Michelle or pull at the bobbles in her hair she says she's fetching Michael.

It's great. The four of us don't touch the ball much but we chase around after the older boys. The score is 5–5 and it's nearly the end of break. I'm dying to get a proper touch so instead of racing around like the others I stand still for a minute. Michael Campbell is running with the ball with all the other kids bouncing off him, but I see that he knocks it too far in front of him so I run in to tackle him. Usually, if you try to tackle Michael Campbell, he bangs you over but my legs are strong from standing up all the time and my dad and uncle Johnny have shown me how to tackle when we play at home. I get my foot to the ball and step through it, all my weight moving forward. I feel Michael's foot behind the ball on the other side but then it gives way. He crashes into my shoulder and then down onto the playground. All the other kids come racing towards the ball so I turn my body so they can't get to it, like I've seen players do on the telly, and wait, wait, wait, because I know Jermaine will run for the ball somewhere. Then there he is, in the corner of my eye, and I pass the ball with the inside of my foot, instead of booting it, and even though it's a bit flat, it rolls, rolls, evenly down the slope in the direction of Top Church and the brewery, and into Jermaine's path. Jermaine knocks it towards Rodney near the goal but I've taken off again and am chasing to get level with him. Rodney tries to flick it in, he's already scored five goals, but their keeper, Mani Singh, stretches out a leg and pokes the ball out to where I'm running. I keep going and hit it full pelt through the posts and into the fir trees that stop the ball going into the road. Mani trips me up after I shoot and I tumble over and tear the knees of my trousers and everyone shouts Goal! Goal! Goal! All my team huddle in front of the goal. The bell goes for the end of break. Michael Campbell is still lying in the middle of the playground like he's dead. He gets up slowly as the classes get into lines and starts to walk towards me.

He's gonna kill yer, Paul and Jermaine say.

We can have him, Ronnie says and takes off his glasses.

Michael doesn't want to fight, though. He stretches out his hand to shake mine and says, Played.

I can see Michelle watching from the girls' line.

Yow lot play again at dinner, Rodney shouts over to us. We do a little dance to celebrate and get told off by Miss Wright.

I remember standing in the class line and looking down at my ragged trousers and closing my eyes and thinking about that feeling when the ball came to me and I banged it in the goal. I still think of it sometimes. When I opened my eyes Michelle was looking over and smiling.

'We don't mind hard work –
and we expect to be rewarded
accordingly. We strive to put
a bit by – and see it grow. Our
aim is to stand on our own
feet, to do the best we can for
our families, and if possible
to ensure that our children
have wider opportunities and
better prospects than we had
ourselves.'

Well, this is just more work in less time, ay it? My grandad studies a piece of paper with my dad at the kitchen table while my nan makes them a cup of tea.

My dad shrugs.

Greater efficiency? Some of the words they use, I ask yer. More work in less time. Next thing ull be more work in less time, for less money, with fewer blokes.

My grandad is laughing but I can tell he doesn't think anything is very funny.

They must think we was all born yesterday.

There ay much yer can do about it, my dad says and shrugs again.

My grandad looks at him over the paper, looks into him. He doesn't say anything. There is something in my grandad's voice, like he knows about who my dad voted for, that makes me worry.

Continental working practices, my grandad reads from the piece of paper.

At least it means there's work, my dad says.

Oh, there's work, there's work.

My grandad leans forward across the kitchen table, over the letter, with his reading glasses in his hand, like he is weighing something up, reckoning.

Well, we cor stop mekkin steel, cor stop mekkin things

altogether. We'll be in a mess then. They said anything
else at yower place?

Short-time, some on em.

Not yow?

All hours, me. My dad grins. They wanna keep the
machines running.

Yow wanna get em payin yer by the hour, our kid, I tell yer.

They are back to normal now. I know what they're
talking about. My grandad gets paid every week, with
his money in an envelope, with a piece of paper that tells
him how much work he's done and how much he's been
paid for it. My dad gets paid every month. He gets paid
the same no matter how often the machines break down.
That's why my nan and grandad pay rent and we pay a
mortgage. We used to pay rent, when my dad got paid
every week in an envelope. This is how it works. If you
get paid monthly you have to start paying money to buy
a house. That's why we live in Elm Drive.

There ay much we can do about it, is there? Keep work-
ing, I suppose, my dad says.

They'll keep us working, yer can be sure of that. My
grandad is looking at him again, working something out,
reckoning, I can see.

My nan puts the tea down on the table.

Continental working practices, my grandad says to her.

He looks at the piece of paper again and then up at my
dad. My dad leans back in the chair, his eyes closing. He
always falls asleep when he comes back from work.

More work in less time, my grandad said. Thass all that is.
He screws the paper up and dips a ginger biscuit in his tea.

More work in less time for less money next. Yow watch.
Yow watch what happens. Yow watch what's coming.

57

I don't think Thatcher knew fully what was coming, from what I understand now, lurching from crisis to crisis in that first year or so, seeing all those *Don't Blame Me, I Voted Labour* stickers, looking like she didn't know what she was doing. There was no plan. Not then. They made a plan up as they went along when they realized we were weaker than they'd imagined. It was opportunistic. All I know is that my grandad could see trouble coming better than anyone else. He knew trouble was coming and he knew there was nothing he could do about it. He knew how weak we were.

But what is a revolution, though?

Johnny explains things to me. He wants there to be a revolution. He tells me about it at the park. I am hanging from the climbing frame, practising for a game we play where we all hold on, legs dangling and hands burning. The winner is whoever lasts the longest. You have to be hard to win. Michelle is the champion. I want to beat her. I am watching a train being shunted in the freight yard down the hill below us.

Well, the way things am shared out ay right.

What dyer mean?

Johnny is sitting with his back to me on the bench. He isn't looking down at the train, he's looking across to the castle and the zoo and is drawing the cable-cars. In his picture the cable-cars hang across to Kates Hill and up the High Street to Top Church and down Castle Hill to Dudley Port station. Imagine, riding around everywhere by cable-car. The patterns the cables make on the page are the same pattern as the cobwebs; that's how Johnny got the idea.

Well, say me, my dad and your dad, we work in factories but the stuff we make is for other people and we don't own the factories, someone else does, well in a way we own Cinderheath, we all do, the people, but it's complicated, so we do all this stuff for someone else who doesn't have to do any of the work.

You get paid.

We do get paid but we don't decide how much pay we get. Someone else decides. If the people who worked in the factories were in charge of them they could work for each other, share things out equally. The way we've got it now, the rich will get richer and the poor will stay poor.

What am we?

What?

Rich or poor?

Well, we'm the workers, the poor, if yer like. We have to rise up and free ourselves.

I'm not sure that we are poor. My grandad is doing loads of overtime at Cinderheath. I can see the works from the climbing frame, over the other side of the railway tracks, the long factory buildings and the gantry that looks like a giant climbing frame above it. Overtime makes you rich. My mum and dad bought our house with his wages and my dad is always at work and sometimes he has to go on the phone or to work even in the middle of the night to tell the people there what to do, how to fix a machine or set it up to cut the steel into shapes. Then there is the business of buying a new house further away from here that I'm not meant to know about. There are poor people but they're not us, I don't think. We've got cars and telephones and we're going to the caravans three times this year. My nan gives money to the poor people in Africa and the Philippines in an envelope that she keeps by the door ready for Sister Marie Antoinette. She shows me pictures of the little children on the envelope and says how we're very lucky. Johnny doesn't make much sense to me, saying we're poor.

This was the first time he explained it to me. Afterwards, I came to see what he meant. We weren't poor, though. Not then, anyway. If you ask me now, I'd say there are lots of ways of making people poor. It's not only about money. Thinking life is only about money is another way of being poor, a way of thinking you might arrive at by counting your coppers in your mean and draughty grocer's shop, looking across the flat Lincolnshire land towards the hills and hating us.

Doh talk so saft. Yome bloody yampy, my grandad says when Johnny starts telling him about the workers and the revolution.

It'll never happen here, son. We get just enough crumbs from the bosses' tables, doh yow worry about that. Just enough. And we'm grateful.

I can't tell if my grandad's joking or not. He looks a bit like he did when punched Uncle Eric.

Johnny blows his cheeks out.

Mind you, my grandad says, there's one or two round here I wouldn't mind being lined up against that wall and shot, when yer get started, like. Yer bloody uncle Eric, for one. He says this last bit quietly so my nan can't hear.

There yer go then!

But it woh, happen, Johnny. People am happy enough as they am. Yer doh know yome born, really, when yer

talk about folks having it really bad. It day happen in the
twenties or thirties, when my dad went hungry, hungry. If
it day happen in the twenties or thirties it ay gonna happen
now. And times afower that. It woh happen now.

  It ay about me. Iss about the system.

  What system? We've got a welfare state, a National
Health Service. We own the bloody steelworks and the
mines. They'm nationalized industries. Who am these
bosses who'm ripping us off? Weselves?

  In a way. The system's wrong.

  Well, the world's unfair, son, I know that much. A revo-
lution woh change that. The system we've got now is a lot
fairer than we have had, believe me.

  Watch what happens. Just watch.

  Then my mum and dad come in from looking for our
new house. But I'm not meant to know about it, so we
talk about the Wolves while they have a cup of tea.

They liked watching cowboy films, my dad and grandad.
They'd watch one together sometimes, say on a Sunday
afternoon: My Darling Clementine, She Wore a Yellow
Ribbon, Shane. I remember one time, when I was really
young, I pretended we were out in Indian territory looking
for that girl; The Searchers was one of my favourite films.
We were over at Kinver or Enville, somewhere like that. I
gave everyone parts as we walked along.

  Who's Johnny gonna be? my mum asked.

  One of the bloody Indians, my grandad said. I remember
they'd had an argument about another cowboy film a few
weeks before.

  Thass all right, is it? Shooting all these people? Johnny
had said.

What? They'm the baddies.

It ay right though, is it?

What ay right? I'm trying to watch this.

Well, just killing em all. That's what really happened. It was their country and then the white men came and killed em all and took the land for theerselves.

Way of the world, son.

So that's all right then, is it, killing women and children?

It's a film.

It really happened.

Let him enjoy the film, Johnny, please, my mum said. Stop worrying about it. It's only a film.

Yer doh understand, Johnny said.

Everyone ignored him and the cavalry charged. I had some plastic cowboys and Indians that I played with Little Ronnie sometimes. I used to make him have the Indians.

Propaganda, Johnny said.

Jesus Christ, iss just a film, son.

The Indians fired arrows through the circled wagons and whooped with delight.

What about *Zulu*? Yer support the Zulus, yer want them to win in that.

Thass different. I doh like Michael Caine.

Or the British Empire. You told me that.

They'm films, son.

You tell me all this stuff, how not to believe what yer see or hear, and then when I repeat it back to yer, yer tell me I'm wrong.

Ah well, maybe it's me yer shouldn't listen to, then.

They still go on like this at times, watching the news. My grandad is almost ninety; Johnny is in his fifties.

My dad liked Clint Eastwood, too. I remember him staying up to watch *A Fistful of Dollars* and drink a bottle of
beer. This was before video or anything like that. He had
that same straight face where you didn't know if he was
joking or angry or what.

The other night, after clearing up in the bar, I poured
a glass of the good rum that Michael had brought back
from Jamaica for me, flicked through the channels. There
he was, suddenly, on the big screen: Clint Eastwood, walking through the desert, looking smaller and smaller as the
empty plains stretched out around him. I changed channel,
tried to think of something else.

When I first bought the pub there were kids selling gear
out of the back room, where the pool table was. They were
in one Tuesday afternoon, there was never anybody else
in, a few weeks after I'd taken it on. I knew I had to do
something. I got Michael to sit at the end of the bar then
I walked in there with a hammer. I said they could leave
now by the side door and never come back or go out the
front in an ambulance. They looked at me and then at
Michael, the infamous Michael Campbell, and left.

Michelle wasn't very pleased with me. Yow think yome
bloody Clint Eastwood, she said. Except he day have his
brother-in-law out on bail, ready to back him up.

Me brother-in-law?

Yer know what I mean.

So you want to marry me, then?

'The choice facing
the nation is between
two totally different
ways of life.'

*Johnny takes me to see Star Wars again. It's back on at
Dudley pictures. I've seen it three times now, once with
my dad, once with my grandad, who fell asleep before they
even left Tatooine, and now with Johnny. Darth Vader
terrifies me but I keep looking. Each time I see it I think
there's no way they can destroy the Death Star, the odds are
too much, the Empire too powerful, but they keep going
and keep going and there it is, a supernova, as the space
station explodes, the rebels have won and good triumphs
over evil, and we come out onto Castle Hill.*

*Johnny wants to paint the enclosures at the zoo. He takes
me there after the film. The man on the turnstile stares at
the red and yellow Anti-Nazi League patch on his arm, and
says, God help us if there's a war, as we shuffle through
to look at the flamingos.*

*I want him to draw the animals. He's got a copy of a
painting of the birdhouse in his sketchbook at home by
Percy Shakespeare, an artist who came from Dudley. The
copy of the picture is black and white, ripped from a book,
but Johnny's gone over it with colours. It's a great painting. I want him to paint something like that, but he tells
me about the animal houses instead.*

*Yeah, the man who built the zoo, he wanted to build a
model city. What that means is a city to show people how*

to live. Even though all the buildings are for animals, he tried to show us how we should build things for humans. Nobody cares about it no more. That's why I'm taking photos and I'm going to paint them, so there's a record of them.

He takes a photo with the Polaroid camera that my uncle Freddie left as a present when he came from Australia. I got a boomerang. Johnny tried painting outside down by the canal with an easel and oil paints. He wanted to paint Cobb's Engine House down at Bumble Hole. That was when the skinheads came and smashed his easel. Now he uses the camera to take pictures and paints with water-colours on the kitchen table or in his room.

The skinheads hang around down near the canal tunnel, sniffing glue and drinking cider. There are punks as well, but you don't see them with the skinheads. There's a punk with blue hair who lives opposite the school and we all run to the fence to laugh at him when he walks past to buy the paper.

My grandad tried to fix the easel but Johnny said, Leave it, Dad. Johnny told me it was like when the Impressionists tried to paint outside and people hated them for it or when Van Gogh was in the Borinage.

I can't follow half of what he's saying. I've never thought of the zoo as a city of animals before but I like the idea of it. Johnny takes photos as we walk round. He's not interested in the animals, just the lines of concrete on the buildings around the hill. I want to go and see the giraffes and the tarantulas in their glass cases. Once I leaned my face to the glass of what I thought was an empty tank, trying to work out if there was anything there, and the spider that I hadn't seen sprang up on its thick back legs *and pressed itself against the glass, two legs feeling for me; it moved like a strange hand, trying to sting, that thin glass between us. I shouted and the guard came and told me off and walked me out to my mum who was waiting outside with an ice cream.*

It's late, the zoo's nearly empty. I hear whooping sounds from round the hill. I wonder if the animals call to each other when there are no humans here.

This is the best one, Sean, look at the curves. There'd been a quarry here, so Lubetkin, that's the man who designed it, had to fit his design into the space where it had been. That was another thing about the way he had to build, he had to fit it all in with the castle and with the quarries and caves. This hill's hollow, you know.

The zoo almost closed during those years. It didn't in the end, about the only thing that didn't. It was like a plague had come. It was what you'd do, I suppose, if you had a plan, if you set out to destroy a place: close the big works first, one by one, create waves that spread out from their closing, factory after factory, shop after shop; later on the brewery, the rail yard, passenger trains had long since finished, even the football ground, the cricket ground, which both slid into the old limestone workings. Johnny was right about the hill being hollow, a whole town was disappearing, caving in.

If you had a plan, you'd tell people they're no good, finished, if they haven't got a job, right after you've taken theirs from them; tell them they're no good if they don't own their house and then try to sell their house back to them; tell them that all that really matters are houses and cars and money, as theirs begin to slip away from them.

You'd set people against each other, some of them will applaud what you are doing, some of them will want their thirty pieces of silver or pay you yours, depending on who the betrayer is – it's not always clear, after all. Some people will do very well, and that's what you'd understand and exploit.

You'd sell off everything else they own, have their schools make them more stupid, have their hospitals make them more sick, never give in, never surrender, make your attack as unrelenting as your voice across the radio and television, telling people how they're no good, explaining to them with concern, and in your brittle fake-posh accent, how you are going to destroy them and there is nothing at all they can do about it.

That's what you'd do, I suppose, if you set out to ruin a place. The zoo was saved; we go there sometimes on summer Sunday afternoons. I tell our children that the animals call to each other when no one's there, that they stroll through their concrete city on the hill. The animals kept their houses and jobs.

The shouts I could hear have got louder, echoing down the hill. They're not animal cries.

Johnny Marsh! a voice shouts across the bear pit. A figure comes out of the trees and down the hill. Two other figures come behind him. They're not walking on the path but straight down the steep bank. You're not meant to; you should stay on the path. They're skinheads. The one in front has got his arms out wide and is holding a big bottle of cider. It's Steven Cooper. He used to be my uncle Johnny's best mate when they were kids. They had a falling out.

Johnny Marsh, fancy seeing yow here! Steve walks along the front of the bear enclosure. You're not meant to do that, either; you might fall in. His two mates walk along the path now, so they come up behind us. I can see straight away that Johnny is worried because he's trying to push the camera in his pocket in a hurry but it's too big and bulky and won't go in.

All right, Steve, he says quietly.

Johnny Marsh. Fancy that. I ay sid yer for donkeys, mate.

I sid yer at the canal, Johnny says.

I can tell Steve's drunk because his eyes aren't looking at Johnny properly.

Less have a picture, John. Doh put yer camera away.

The other two have come round to us. I can see they're drunk too.

Paulie, Yvette, look who's here. Iss Johnny Marsh.

One of them is a girl. I've never seen a girl skinhead before. She's got blue eye make-up on and a bit of hair that twirls down her back but the rest of her hair is shaved and she's wearing Dr Marten boots and a V-neck jumper.

Look at him, she says and points at me. Ay he lovely. Woss his name, John?

Sean, I say. Me name's Sean.

Woss he? Yer boyfriend, eh, John? Bit young, mate, Steve says.

Me nephew, Johnny says.

I want him to say fuck off. That's what I've heard the bigger boys say when this kind of thing happens. Well, only twice really, once when everyone thought Michael Campbell was going to beat Rodney James up and Rodney told him to fuck off and then Michael didn't do anything and then a second time when everyone thought Michael

69

*was going to beat up Mani Singh and Mani said fuck off
and then Michael beat him up anyway.*

*I think of saying it. I try to force it from my mouth.
There's going to be a fight.*

*Could do with his hair cut, the one called Paulie says.
He looks like Steve, maybe his brother, but his hair's cut
even shorter so his head looks blue, like it's been shaded
with one of Johnny's pastels. He's got the beginnings of a
tattoo on his neck and a spider's web on his elbow.*

Less have a picture, Johnny, come on, eh.

*The three of them stand posing, leaning on the railing
of the bear pit; the bear somewhere below them. There is
no one else around.*

*Dyer wanna come in the picture, Sean? the girl says.
Now's a chance to say fuck off but I don't. I just stand
there.*

*Johnny says, Goo on, Sean, dyer wanna get in the
picture?*

*He jerks his head for me to pose with them. I've never
seen him like this. He looks down at the ground and his
hair hangs in his eyes. If he fought thirty of them down
by the canal he could easy fight these three now.*

*Maybe he's playing along with them. Maybe he's going to
kick them over the railing into the bear pit. I don't know
why he wants me in the way. I want to run. I know there
is trouble coming.*

Johnny takes a picture and they all grin.

Yvette says, Smile, Sean, and I try to smile.

Lovely. Good picture, Johnny?

*Johnny nods and looks down at the camera. I swear his
hands are shaking. He holds the picture and waits for it
develop.*

Yer gooin up the Wolves this year, Johnny?

Johnny nods.

And away?

Some wiks. I work some Saturday mornings so it depends.

Good lad, Steve says. It's funny how he says that, like he's older than Johnny even though they're the same age.

Our faces appear from the photo's white mist. I look happy in the picture, like I've just met long-lost friends. They can go now.

Good lad, Sean. Could do with that hair cut, though. Yer enjoying yer trip to the zoo, eh, Sean?

This is Steve again. His eyes look right into me.

I nod.

Arr, an me.

He pulls three ten-pence pieces out of his pocket and holds them out to me and says, Get yerself an ice cream, son.

I don't know what to do.

Come on, Sean, where's yer manners?

I open my hand and take the money. Thanks, I say.

Good lad.

Paulie leans forward and touches Johnny's camera.

This is a lovely camera, Johnny. Can I have a look?

Johnny lets him take it; opens his hands and lets him lift it out of them.

I think, Please do something, Johnny, please, and almost straight away realize he isn't going to, so I hope that a zookeeper comes along quickly, or someone, anyone. I've never been to the zoo when it hasn't been busy.

I hear the elephant trumpeting from up the hill.

Steve leans in now, touches the sleeve of Johnny's jacket; that badge with Anti-Nazi League written on it.

What's this, Johnny, eh? What's this?

Johnny doesn't say anything.

The other two have taken a few steps away from us. They've got the camera. I realize they are stealing it as Steve says, Oh, yer saft cunt, really quietly, gently almost, and then leans back and takes a step away before he punches Johnny quick and hard so you could almost not realize it has happened and Johnny staggers backwards into me.

Steve strolls away from us and joins the other two and they pick up their pace a little bit, look up the path, maybe they see someone coming. Paulie holds the camera up in the air and Yvette blows us a kiss before they turn and hurry round the corner and into the trees, and I hear their whooping and shouting again.

Johnny's nose bleeds across the concrete. He holds the sleeve of his jacket to it with his head bowed. You're meant to hold your head back for a nose bleed, I want to tell him; that's what they make Little Ronnie do at school. I've got the thirty pence in my hand. I stick it in my pocket.

You okay? he says, leaning against the railing, bleeding.

Yeah, I say. Yeah. I am. I'm fine.

He was right about Lubetkin, who'd built that shining city on a hill for the animals to live in. Someone told me that before Lubetkin arrived the Earl of Dudley wanted to keep the animals in mock-castles to match the one on top of the hill, instead he got a city of the future: socialist, concrete, pure and clean.

While they built the zoo, this is in the mid-thirties, they cleared the centre of the town and moved the people to the new estates, spiralling out from the castle: shining new cities of their own, with broad streets named after birds, trees and flowers and houses with kitchens and neat, brick toilets.

I want to ask Johnny why he didn't fight them, but I don't say anything. We walk home. Johnny doesn't say anything either. I mean not one word all the way. Usually, you can't stop him talking. He holds his sleeve to his nose and it stops bleeding as we cross the Birmingham New Road. There's blood all up the sleeve of his jacket. People look at him. He walks me back to our house as he's agreed with my mum.

Doh say nothing to anyone, Sean, abaht this afternoon, all right?

No, okay, I say.

He waits at the end of the path and sees me walk to the front door.

Yer not coming in, John? my mum calls to him down the path. He's already halfway to the main road.

Nah, I've gorra get back, he says and my mum looks confused.

Did yer have a nice time? my mum asks me. Enjoy the film?

It was great, I say, trying not to burst into tears, forcing myself not to say anything. It's a great film. I love Star Wars.

Is Johnny all right?

Yeah, I said, course he is.

Did yer say thank you?

When I ran away for the second time it was to Mos Eisley, that bar at the start of *Star Wars*, the pirate city, where Han

Solo shoots someone; the edge of an empire where it frays and unravels. That's what it feels like now. I ran away to sea, worked on the cruise ships for seven, eight years while my mum drank herself to death in the room I fell from. I only came back for the very end. Deep down, I knew it was too late. I should never have left in the first place.

When you live in the middle of England, the sea is like a dream. It's there in the rocks, trilobites that floated here millions of years ago, lying there inside the hills, but nowhere to be seen. I used to stand on Cawney Bank and kid myself I could see the sea, tried to look down all through Worcestershire and Gloucestershire, down the long banks of the Severn, to the muddy estuary glittering there way beyond the horizon.

Mos Eisley actually exists. The film-set is in the Tunisian desert, a mirage, the greedy sands of the Sahara beyond it. I went there once when we had a few days stay in Sidi Bou Saïd. Cairo, Kingston, Tangier: when I worked on the ships I'd always search out somewhere like it, bars in Naples, Liverpool, New York, places where people wash up when they've got nowhere else to go. You get them everywhere, though. I needn't have sailed the seven seas. I own one, live in one now myself; carry it with me like Albert the tortoise and his painted shell. Dudley is the frayed edge of an empire, after all.

'From France to the Philippines, from Jamaica to Japan, from Malaysia to Mexico, from Sri Lanka to Singapore, privatization is on the move . . . The policies we have pioneered are catching on in country after country.'

I watch my dad change after work. He wears a shirt with a tie on underneath his overalls now he has his new job. I sit on the bed as he pulls an old shirt from the drawer. I wish he'd been at the zoo. He'd have killed them. I want to tell him about it but something holds me back. Maybe it's better not to say anything. The way he sits with his shirt off makes me think of when he used to play football. He worked at the Drop Forge then and that was the name of the team too. My grandad would walk me over there, for the second half usually, I was five. Johnny would meet us on his bike. They wore old gold shirts, like the Wolves.

Come on, Drop Forge, my dad would say and clap his hands after he'd headed the ball, and he'd say get out, out, when they cleared it and he got the defence to move up. The best was when Drop Forge got a corner and he would jog up the pitch to the other team's goal and the players would say, Goo on, Francis. One time we'd taken Ronnie as well and my dad went up for two corners in a row and both times the ball came swinging across the trees and he ran in and headed it hard past the keeper. The second goal, he knocked one of their players into the net as well. It was a cup game. I remember we went to the door of the changing rooms at the end and my dad was sitting on the wooden bench with his shirt off holding a can of beer, laughing; all the shirts were in a pile on the floor in front of the players and everyone was talking at once and steam came drifting from the showers. He doesn't play any more, because of work, I think.

What dyer do at school today, Sean?

I day go to school, I went to the pictures and the zoo with Johnny.

Say don't, Sean. Yer shouldn't miss school.

His face is serious, looking in the mirror on the wardrobe door with his shirt crumpled in his lap.

Iss the holidays, I say.

He looks blankly at me in the mirror.

We'm gooin to the caravans on Saturday. I say this in a panic. He can't have forgotten we're going on holiday, can't have. There's a suitcase at the side of the bed. I can see my mum's summer tops waiting in there.

Oh, right, he says, and starts to pull his shirt on and grins at me in the mirror.

Dad, I say, and the relief rushes through my stomach and down into my legs. He reaches out and ruffles my hair and everything is all right.

What did yer see at the pictures?

Star Wars.

Again? Was there nothing else on?

I wanted to see it again.

All set for next week, then?

Yeah.

Have yer put the cricket stuff ready, the football, anything else yer want to take?

I nod. It's all set by the garage door.

Good. I'm looking forward to it, sunshine. He lies back on the bed. I cor wait. He closes his eyes for a moment.

77

Yer should go to school, though, Sean. I never did, son, and look at me.

Then the phone rings and it's my dad's boss and my dad talks to him for a bit, then he goes back out to work. My mum puts his tea back in the cooker to keep it warm. She's not very pleased and says this has got to stop. When my dad gets back the gravy's gone all thick and he wipes it around the plate with his bread.

Iss gonna mek yer ill, all this back and forth, my mum says.

Iss all right, my dad says. Everything'll be all right.

I thought my dad was joking about not going to school but it turned out that he hardly did. He'd done jobs for his uncles when he was a kid. Up at Quarry End, where they lived, no one was ever that particular about going to school. His dad was dead, his brothers all much older and moved away. They worked on the roads, labouring, that kind of thing. A couple of them worked on farms out towards Worcester. None of them settled after Quarry End was blown up.

I lie on the short, tough grass in front of the caravans with my shirt pulled up around my neck so that the grass tickles my body. The grass is strong and prickly from being eaten by the sheep and from the wind blowing in off the sea. I can hear the waves now, crunching up the beach, but I'm looking the other way, at my dad sitting in a deckchair in front of the caravan dipping a biscuit in a cup of tea. The sun is behind our caravans and the big hills are black and solid behind that. In the morning they look like mountains, with the sun behind them, all in shadow, like you would never want to go there, only on an adventure not on your holiday, then in the afternoon they look like hills again, soft and green, with sheep dotted around them and grey cottages here and there. One time we saw a hare run across one of the fields, its long shadow running next to it. A kestrel hung still in the sky, hanging there; watching the hare run.

My dad looks out to sea. He has a moustache now. My grandad says he looks like Dennis Lillee, the Australian bowler. When he bowls to us on the beach he runs in hard and fast and then sends the ball in a gentle arc so that we might hit it.

He's out of the deckchair, springing to his feet, and he's got his arm round me, pointing, pointing, out at sea.

Look, can yer see it? A porpoise, look! Jumping out the water, look, theer it goes again! Yer see?

I nod and pretend I can see it. I look across the grey blanket of the sea. The water looks still and empty to me, but I want to say I've seen it. I'm not that sure what a porpoise looks like. I don't want to disappoint my dad. This feeling fills me and I can't see anything. He pulls me close to him.

Yeah, yeah, I can see it, I say and try to follow the line of where he's pointing. I see it, I say.

I can't. I know we are looking at different things.

When I worked on the ships I used to lift my eyes to the horizon and scan the water, looking for porpoises breaking the surface. I didn't see any then, either. It was too late, anyway. We saw dolphins a few times, whole families of them. One morning, we were near Madeira, a whale surfaced alongside the ship next to the bar where I was cleaning the glasses. It kept coming and coming, rolling through the water, this grooved, blue-black flesh rolling through the water, blotches of shellfish in tiny clusters on its flank, and it came rolling, rolling, through the water. It blew this explosion of air, hard, from its blowhole, rolling then out of the water, the same air that we breathe that had been inside this whale and down to the depths of the ocean, and the spray made a rainbow on the sea's surface. I could see Madeira there on the horizon, jutting out of the sea, like another whale emerging. Then the whale's tail, the fluke, rose up out of the water, black against the shining ocean, and slapped down hard on the surface, not graceful, clumsy even, and the water displaced then swirled in after the whale and it had gone, with the sea moving up and down, up and down; the whale heading down to the depths and the sea becoming slowly still like nothing had ever been there. I thought, Can you see it, Dad? Can you see this? As if it was me holding onto him and looking out across the water. Full fathom five thy father lies, I thought. Those are the pearls. And I carried on looking at the empty sea and shelving the glasses in the freezer so they would keep the beer cold. I thought about my dad's eyes. A passenger came and ordered his first of the day. He hadn't seen the whale either.

They're not our caravans. They don't belong to us, that is, but we come to the same ones every year. We have one and my nan and grandad live in the one next to us and Uncle Johnny stays in there too sometimes. He comes on the train because his holiday is different. He has to fit in with the other workers. We go and meet him and pick him up at Porthmadog and drop him off when he is leaving.

*We have the cars. If we go anywhere in the car then my
dad and grandad get the maps out and lay them on the
car roofs before we set off or look at them on the table
the night before, even though we always drive to the same
places and they know the way: Beddgelert, round Snowdon
and past the lakes to Llanberis, to Porthmadog to the train
station and shops, Criccieth for ice cream and so on.*

*I look at the maps with them, try to say the Welsh names
and then look at all the spaces on the map where no one
lives. If you look at a map of home there are hundreds
of streets all together, then spaces for the factories and
sometimes the hills, and canals criss-crossing the map.
Here there aren't many streets, just hills and farms, green
and brown outlines, and sometimes castles and streams
and rivers that twist across the map because of the shape
of the hills, not like with our canals where you have a
tunnel or a lock so the canal carries on in a straight line,
just built through whatever was there.*

One year all the Robertsons came. They stayed all in one
caravan, their mum and dad and six kids plus Natalie's
little baby.

Never again, we might as well stop at home, my nan said.

I thought it was great.

*I go with Ronnie down to the rock pools and collect things.
He keeps a pet crab in a bucket for a few days. I tell him to
walk it on a lead. One hot afternoon I lie on the rough grass
and can see underneath our caravan through to Ronnie's
mum sitting smoking in her shorts and drinking from a
glass with ice melting in it that Ronnie's dad has walked
over from the club with, laughing because you're not meant*

to take glasses away. I know I shouldn't be looking at her. She pulls the shoulder straps of her top down and I can see where her skin is lighter there and dark brown on her arms and shoulders. She's tied her wavy black hair up on top of her head. I think of the drawings of Natalie hidden in Johnny's sock drawer.

Six kids, older than me, rough as you like, and looking like that, I hear my mum say to my nan.

Ah, it only brings trouble, my nan says.

Here's to you, Mrs Robertson.

Mrs Robinson, ay it?

That was a joke, Mother, my mum says.

The main reason for going on holiday is for my dad and grandad to have a rest from work. My grandad says that when he retires, which is a few years away yet, or if he wins the pools, then he'd like to get a bungalow here. There's a row of them as you walk away from the sea and down the lane towards Llanystumdwy. Whenever he talks about it my nan rolls her eyes like she doesn't want it to happen. She says she prefers it for a holiday. I'd like to live here, though, in the caravans, as long as we all stay.

Some people live in caravans all the time, I say to Ronnie.

Yeah, the gypos, he says.

When they knocked all the old houses down on Kates Hill the gypsies came and lived there. They lived in caravans and drove lorries. We were told not to go near them because they were dirty. People said they had a disease where you have to keep going to the toilet, called dysentery. I told my mum this while she was ironing and she said not to believe everything I heard, but to stay away anyway. I thought it was funny how everyone said the gypsies were

82

dirty because they lived in caravans, then went and lived in a caravan for their holidays. I told my mum this and she laughed, but then she said maybe not to say that outside the house as not everybody thought the same as we did.

You mean like Margaret Thatcher? I said.

Exactly.

Why doh we think the same as Margaret Thatcher?

Well, she's not a very nice person. Say don't, not doh.

Why?

So people outside Dudley can understand what yer say to them.

No, why is Margaret Thatcher not a nice person?

She's not kind. She doesn't care about people.

She's selfish.

Exactly, she's very selfish.

If we doh think the same as Margaret Thatcher why's her in charge? Why doh we have somebody in charge who we do like?

Well, some people like her. I'd have thought Johnny would've gone through all this with you.

She smiled as she said this. She knew that Johnny wanted there to be a revolution and she thought it was a ridiculous idea. I wanted to say, Does Dad like her? Then if she said, no, I could have said, Why did he vote for her, then? and if she said Yes, I could ask why. If I had said that, though, she would have realized that I listened to them talking in the kitchen while I sat on the stairs above them. My mum put the iron down on the ironing board.

That's why we have an election. So people can decide who they want. The people picked Margaret Thatcher as prime minister. Why am yer so interested in this, Sean?

What people?

All the people vote. Different areas vote for MPs.
Margaret Thatcher's party the Conservatives have got
the most MPs so she's prime minister. Some people doh
think the same as us. Some people am different to us.
Don't worry about it.

Like the gypos?

Don't you dare say gypos! I doh want to hear you say-
ing that word!

She pointed her finger right in my face; this was one step
away from getting a whack.

I said I was going to the Paki shop once because I'd heard
Paul say it and thought it sounded good. My mum slapped
me and as I tried to duck her engagement ring cut my
eyebrow and blood spattered red on the kitchen lino. My
mum burst into tears before the blood hit the floor. I still
have a tiny scar. I never said it again.

You can call them gypsies. I don't want you repeating what
you hear other people say.

She says this all the time.

Actually, I have heard my dad call them gypos when he
was washing the car, talking to a neighbour of ours called
Mick, but I think I'd better not mention it. He'd said it
about the Robertsons, so maybe that was different.

Like the gypsies then?

No, not like the gypsies. I don't suppose they voted. They
might not be able to vote.

I thought everyone could vote if you're over eighteen.
You told me.

You have to be registered.

This is complicated.

I doh know why yome so worried about it, Sean. It's nothing for you to worry about. I'm gonna tell Johnny and yer grandad to stop talking about politics, putting ideas in yer head.

What about Jermaine's dad?

What about him?

Maybe he likes Margaret Thatcher.

What?

You said not everybody is the same as us. And the Campbells.

She starts to laugh.

Oh, Sean. I shouldn't have thought Jermaine's dad or the Campbells was that keen on Margaret Thatcher. They'm West Indian, black, it's not different. You might hear some people say that they'm different, though. I'm talking about people that think differently, not people with a different coloured skin.

But who, though?

Who what?

Thinks different to us?

Well, Margaret Thatcher, for one and yer uncle Eric. You heard all the fuss.

And my dad, I want to add.

Am we rich or poor?

Are we rich or poor? Why are you asking this now? I've told you, no more politics.

Would you say we'm rich or poor?

I'd say we're very lucky.

Rich, then?

No, Sean, not rich. We're not rich, no; just richer than we used to be. Ask your grandad, but no more politics.

She was thirty that year. My dad got Johnny to do a picture of my mum for her birthday. He used pastels and she looked happy in the picture, like when she'd stand in the kitchen on Crow Street and sing along to the radio. She was too embarrassed to put the picture up. My dad had to put it up in the garage. I don't know what happened to it afterwards. We have old photos. There's one that maybe Johnny used as a model that shows her turning her head, standing on the back step, holding me as a baby, my grandad's rose bushes on one side, with shadows angled across the wall. She is about to smile, not quite ready to pose, happy; her eyes are happy.

We went to Stratford and walked by the river, looked at the Shakespeare statues, then we went on a boat and looked into the gardens of the big houses and my mum and dad imagined living there. My mum had long brown hair then; I remember her looking with wonder and anger at a grey hair she pulled from her head. She wore dresses that she made herself with big prints on them like butterflies or flowers. She had made all the curtains and bed covers for our new house and kept material in the cupboard under the stairs along with her sewing machine. When she cleaned at the solicitors, she had to tie her hair back in a ponytail or put it in a net, which she hated. She hated that job. She did it to get some extra money in because we had a mortgage to pay. It was my dad that wanted us to get money together and move again when he got another job.

They'd been married for ten years. I was born nine months after they got married. When I was a baby we'd lived all together at my nan and grandad's, all of us in the back bedroom that I'd fallen out of. We moved to the

Perry Court flats and had a balcony that looked back up to the castle and over all the works at Cinderheath and down towards Tipton. Then we moved to our house the autumn after the baking hot summer.

My dad grew up in Quarry End. It wasn't there any more. They blew it up in a big explosion to join the two quarries together.

Pity they day blow the folks from theer up an all, my uncle Eric had said, before he was banished. Then he said, No offence, Francis, to my dad. I day mean yow.

I remember no one seemed that sad to see Quarry End go except the people who'd clung on there until the end, like my granny, my dad's mum, living in part-demolished terraces with the quarries eating at the foundations of their houses. I liked it. My granny died before they'd have finally moved her out. She had nowhere to go. I remember going up there with my dad. He had to meet his brothers at the house to divide up my granny's stuff. My dad didn't like his brothers. We had to burn most of it; the furniture had woodworm and all the clothes and blankets were too dirty for anything else, not even rag and bone. We all stood round the bonfire and the smoke mixed with the dust that used to come from the blasting and cover everything with a light grey powder. That was what it was like up there, dusty and foggy, so to an eight-year-old boy it felt like monsters might come round the corner of every building. While we had the fire burning a fox came along the road with all her cubs in a line behind her; they were all grey from the dust in their fur. She came right by the fire and the men and sniffed at what was going on. One of my dad's brothers, Harry, I think, who went to live in Worcester, worked on the oil rigs for a time, threw a brick right at it and the fox stood there and stared, like the wild things had taken over.

The road used to wind between the quarries, the new one and the old one, and the houses used to run on either side of the road at the top of the hill. That one narrow road was undermined slowly by the working, so that eventually the back yards of the houses were nearly at the quarry edges. My dad could remember when the new quarry had been much smaller and there'd been a farm with horses where the big hole was now. Although it was just two long lines of terraced houses, Quarry End was a separate place with shops and pubs in the row, and yards out the back where people kept chickens and pigs. I'm not sure my dad's mum, my granny, ever left Quarry End.

People were scared to go up there if they didn't know any of the families. They said you'd get beaten up or killed and thrown over the quarry or fed to the pigs. That didn't really happen. Well, it happened once, which is where the story came from.

A man was walking from Blackheath to visit his sister on Kates Hill and instead of carrying on down Rowley Road or starting through White Heath and then past the Four Ways and up and over to the Hangsman's Tree and that way, he decided to walk up through Quarry End. He didn't know anybody up there and work was slow at the quarries, so the men were stood on the doorsteps and at the door of the pub and because they didn't like the look of the man they started calling him names and hitting him. The man ran off and they chased him, a big group of them now, twenty or thirty, kids and grown men; that was how they did things up there, all together. The man must have been in a panic because he turned off the road down one of the lanes that ran off into the blackberry bushes and chicken coops and he went falling over into the quarry and broke his neck. Some of the gang climbed down and dragged the man out, but they didn't know what to do with the body. The police didn't go much to Quarry End but they'd probably turn up for something like this. So they fed the man from Blackheath to the pigs. The pigs ate him up. The best sausages used to come from Quarry End and after that people used to joke that it was because of what they fed the pigs on. It was no joke, though. The police came from Dudley and found some of the man's bones in the pig trough. Nobody said anything. Nobody got arrested. My dad told me that his dad was one of the boys who did the chasing.

The best days at the caravans are the ones when we don't drive anywhere. I wake up early because the sun comes in through the orange curtains early in the morning and makes the room glow. I lie awake while my nan makes a cup of tea for us all. Sometimes I sleep in our caravan, sometimes in my nan and grandad's. My bed is in the same position in both. I wriggle down the bed a little bit and move the curtain with my feet so I can look out and see the line of the sea and the sky and the tops of the waves. Even when the sun isn't shining it's good. You can watch the grey waves and the seagulls as they fly across the space in the window between the curtain and the window frame. When it's raining it's even better because you can snuggle down in bed and hear the rain hitting the roof and the sound of the kettle boiling and usually the waves are white and foamy and they hit the sea wall and come splashing into the caravan site. If it rains in the day I don't mind.

I sit in the corner and read or write in my exercise book or chat to whoever's around. Some days when it rains we go for a drive and look at the mountains and castles that appear through the mist.

I walk with my dad and grandad to get a paper and anything else we might want for breakfast, like more eggs. The shop for the caravans is part of a farm and the eggs are laid by the chickens that live up the hill. I walk up and see them sometimes. After breakfast we go on another walk along the beach past where the sea wall runs out and there are the rock pools where me and Ronnie caught his pet crab. Afternoons, we all play on the beach in front of the caravans and that's when there's a big game of cricket or football. We go in the sea, if it's hot, and I run back and forth through the waves as they foam up the sand.

'In Britain, we have a tradition of facing the severest tests as a family, working together to meet and overcome adversity.'

She stopped all the little children from having milk.

My mum lifts her head up from the ironing and says this to me while I line up my Star Wars *figures on the table.*

What?

You asked me why Margaret Thatcher was selfish, why we don't like her. When I was a little girl all the children got given milk to drink every morning at school. As soon as Margaret Thatcher was in charge of it, she stopped the milk.

Milk's really good for you.

Exactly.

She must really hate us, I think. You can see if you watch her on telly or even if you hear her voice coming out of the radio that we make her angry. At least, someone makes her angry. Even when she said that Saint Francis stuff, it was like she was telling everyone off. Things are getting out of hand. She wants to stop people going to work, let all the factories close. That's what my grandad says. I want to know why. I don't know what we've done to upset her, but we've done something. If we know why she's angry maybe we can stop her.

Why did she do that, then? Why's she so angry?

That's just what she's like. It's what some people am like, Sean.

So why would people vote for her, then?

Just– I suppose they might think they'll get something out of it themselves.

My mum holds a shirt of my dad's up to the kitchen window to check it's not creased.

What like?

I dunno, Sean. That's enough of that, now. You haven't got to worry about it. I'm sorry I mentioned it.

Like money or a new house?

Well, yeah, I suppose so. My mum blows out her cheeks and looks at the steam rising from the damp shirt. Yeah, that's it exactly, really. Anyway, enough now. Carry on playing with yer little men. Why don't you wanna see if Ronnie wants to come to our house for a change? You only ever play with him when we're up at Nan and Grandad's.

It's funny that I have never thought to ask him. It's as if he only exists on Crow Street.

I don't want Ronnie to come here. I don't like Elm Drive. I don't like the way my room looks out on the trees and nothing else. At my nan and grandad's you can see for miles and there are all sorts of things going on: the factories and allotments and the little cars far away on the motorway and the trains creeping alongside the factory buildings and by the canal as they go into Dudley Port station. I don't like these orange bricks that our house is made with that are all the same; I like the purply-reddy ones on Crow Street where you find things growing or crawling in between them. Ronnie even pulled a brick out of their house once and hid a pound note behind it to stop his sisters finding it. When he collected it there were woodlice living under it like it was a tent. I don't like how quiet it is on our road or that it's a dead end. On Crow Street it's all noise: you can hear everything, like the Robertsons shouting and playing next door, Jennie Lee the budgie, or Barbara Castle, as the new budgie is called, and the birds outside singing, metal clanging from the works, doors slamming, the radio playing, the men calling to each other on the allotments or on their way home from work. Even the car sounds there are different because on our street the sound is of cars that people have turned the key in and started up, cars they bought from a proper garage, but on Crow Street pretty much all the cars belong to Harry Robertson and he tries to fix them up and sell them. There are always cars attached to each other with spark plugs; me and Little Ronnie sit in them sometimes while his dad tries to get them going; or there are cars that Harry is taking apart or trying to put back together. If a car is beyond repair then Charlie Clancey comes along and takes it for the scrapyard. There's always someone to talk to at my nan and grandad's. My nan says it makes her head go round.

In our house I'm on my own. I hear my nan sometimes say that it would be nice if I had a brother or sister to play with. It would, it's true. She's been dropping hints lately, saying things like, Well, there's ten years between yow and Johnny to my mum, doh give up on the idea. I know my mum and dad have tried to grow one loads of times, but they haven't managed to yet. You have to try and grow a baby inside the woman's belly. I don't need Michelle Campbell to tell me that.

Even the garden at our house isn't as good as it seems. We put a swing in it but you can't really see anything while you're swinging, only the fence. I prefer the swings at the park because as you swing you can watch the freight trains coming into the yard and if you go and stand at the wall *you can see them shunting and look at all the different tracks as they criss-cross. You can see the cable-car at the zoo as well and sometimes you can make out the llamas on the side of the hill below the castle and the little splashes of pink that are the flamingos. And there are other kids. I don't say anything, though. It seems important that I have my own swing. When I'm sitting out on the back step at Crow Street, my nan tells me how lucky I am to have such a nice house to go back to. I think, If it's that nice, why are my mum and dad looking at other houses even further away? And why are we always round here? But I don't say anything.*

I know that our house will cause more trouble than it is worth. That's what my grandad says and I believe him.

And in the end that turned out to be true. That house brought more trouble than anything we could have imagined.

'No one would remember
the Good Samaritan if he'd
only had good intentions; he
had money as well.'

Johnny comes in with the paper and my grandad starts on about the Wolves.

A million pound for him?

Million and half, really.

How have they got that much money?

They got the money for Daley.

He's another un. They ay wuth that much, these players.

My grandad stares at the Express & Star. Wolves have bought Andy Gray from Villa. It's great news. My grandad never thinks anyone is any good apart from the players from when Wolves were the best team in the world.

He's a great signing, Dad.

Well, he needs to be Alfredo Di Stéfano for that money.

Iss the way of the world, Jack. Money decides things in the end, my dad says.

Does it? my grandad says. Does it?

He looks at my dad.

Yer know what I mean.

I think my grandad knows how my dad voted.

I think I do, arr. Yow watch what's coming.

I have no idea why my dad voted Tory in 1979. It's true that he wasn't as political as my mum or any of the family but he'd voted Labour before 1979 and he voted Labour afterwards. It was a mistake, I suppose. I don't know what he thought he was going to get from it: houses, money, cars. It was maybe a moment of rebellion; the possibility of stepping away from one life into another, a metamorphosis; the whole country changed. All I know is that he wouldn't have, if he'd known what was going to be unleashed.

At school we learn about the Victorians. Edward Oxford is the name of the man who tried to kill Queen Victoria in 1840. We don't learn about this in school; I found it out at the library after I heard Johnny and my grandad talking about it after there was an article about it in the Black Country Bugle. *Edward Oxford was from Birmingham. Queen Victoria didn't say the insults about the Black Country, didn't ask for the blinds on the royal train to be drawn so she didn't have to look at us, until 1866, though, so it wasn't like he was trying to get revenge for that. She hadn't drawn the blinds on Birmingham, anyway, only on Dudley Port until she got to Wolverhampton, that was what I heard; she said we were too ugly to look at.*

Probably reminded her of where all her money come from, my grandad says when I ask him about it. Keeping her in the manner to which her'd become accustomed, we and a few million Indians, he adds.

She thought Birmingham was okay; it was us she didn't like. Birmingham had a statue of her by the town hall and the museum. The pigeons poo on her and the white poo runs down her face like she's crying, like the statues of Mary in my nan's books on Lourdes and Walsingham.

At his trial at the Old Bailey, Edward Oxford said, I may as well shoot at her as anybody else, and everyone thought he was mad, so they let him go to hospital instead of prison. That was a bit of a let-off for Edward Oxford because he wasn't really mad at all. They decided to let him out of hospital and sent him to Australia, where my uncle Freddie lives. When Freddie came back to visit he brought me a boomerang with koalas on that Aborigines had painted. You used to get sent to Australia if you committed a crime, like the Artful Dodger at the end of Oliver Twist. It was meant to be a punishment and you had to spend weeks on a boat eating bread and water and could never come home again but it didn't seem that bad to me, really. Uncle Freddie had to pay ten pounds to move to Australia.

There are photos in the drawer at my nan and grandad's of Uncle Freddie, Aunty Gloria and their son, Jeff. In the photos there are palm trees and brightly coloured birds in the trees, not in a cage like Jennie Lee or Barbara Castle, and Jeff is a blond-haired boy standing with a cricket bat. They all look very happy in Australia. Uncle Freddie was always happy during his visit here. My nan shows me the pictures and tells me all about it. I ask her if she wants to go and she laughs and says, no way, she belongs in Dudley. Loads of people must have gone to Australia, though, because they needed to fill the whole country up. It looks good to me. If we need to move anywhere we should move to Australia. All countries used to send their criminals away to other places. At the caravan Dad, Grandad and Johnny stay up to watch a film called Papillon *about a man from France who is taken to a tropical island that is also a prison. I can see the television from under the bed covers. The man's name is Papillon, which means butterfly, and he is locked up in solitary confinement and has no food, so he has to eat a centipede that he finds in*

99

his cell. I hear my dad say it's a true story and that he's read the book.

Anyway, that's what happened to Edward Oxford: he got sent to Australia. He even wrote a book about Australia after he'd lived there for a while and been sent to prison for stealing a shirt. I read all this in the library, upstairs at the reference table, not downstairs in the children's section.

Edward Oxford must have had a pretty bad aim because he missed the queen from right up close. He waited behind a tree at the bottom of Constitution Hill, which is near Buckingham Palace. When the queen came along with Prince Albert in their horse and carriage, Edward Oxford stepped out and fired two guns, one in each hand, right at them. He missed both times and that was when he was arrested.

I put my hand up to start explaining all this at school and Mrs Jones, our new teacher, tells me to stop talking.

I had an inkling even then, I think. If things had turned out differently I don't suppose it would have come to anything, it would have remained a thought, unrealized. There was something in the pictures of workhouse children and slums and crowded factories that scared me. I was worried by the darkness of the pictures in the textbook we looked at; a photograph of a boy that Dr Barnardo had found living in a barrel. And by the relish with which Mrs Jones told us that if we'd been Victorians we'd have all been stuffed up chimneys or down mines or buried in a pit at the bottom of the churchyard.

I want to carry on talking and ask Mrs Jones to imagine if Edward Oxford had shot at her. Victoria was quite a new queen then, young. None of the pictures of her looking old with her hair in a bun and her veil, all dressed in black and looking miserable existed yet. The statue wouldn't be there by Birmingham Town Hall. We wouldn't be learning about the Victorians; they'd have been called something else.

There would have been different kings and queens. Or maybe they wouldn't have bothered having a queen at all after Edward Oxford had shot her and we'd have had a revolution and become a republic like Johnny wanted us to be. Maybe on stamps there would be pictures of Edward Oxford, and a statue of him up in Birmingham, his home town, because afterwards maybe everyone would have decided that it was a good idea, to have killed the queen. I know that people are always deciding things are a good idea after they've happened. Quite often people think things are a good idea and then change their minds afterwards, like voting for Margaret Thatcher, for instance.

Well, yow voted for it, my mum says quietly to my dad when a factory closes.

All right, I was wrong.

I could have tode yer that.

Yow have.

I think about how much those one or two shots might have changed things. I look at the picture of the boy in the barrel. He lived in a barrel in an alleyway in the East End of London in the rain and snow and fog. He had to find scraps off the floor to eat, apple cores and cabbage leaves and things that people had left out for the pigs. In the picture he looks strange, his hair all standing on end and his head too big for his body. It says that he died.

If Edward Oxford had killed Queen Victoria then maybe there would have been a big fuss about the state the country *was in and about why he'd killed her because at the time no cared about that little boy in the barrel dying, apart from Dr Barnardo. That was how things got changed. It makes me think. If Margaret Thatcher is causing us all such a problem, why doesn't someone shoot her? Probably, afterwards, people would say that they've done a good thing. Some people would, anyway. It's okay to try to kill evil people, we got told this in assembly, like in the war when we fought the Germans. It's like trying to kill Hitler or when they killed Mussolini in Italy and hung him from a lamp-post. My grandad had fought in Italy in the war. It was where the gun was from. The one that he kept in that rusty box that he'd laid out on the lawn after I broke the shed and then put back in the same place in the new shed.*

I didn't tell anyone about any of this, though. I wasn't stupid. I ran around playing with Ronnie and the others. Most of the time I hadn't got a care in the world. I was only a kid, after all. But there was always something there; some sense that one day we might have to fight back.

Wolves are in the League Cup final against Nottingham Forest. Johnny's got a ticket.

I tode yer he was worth the money, Dad, he says to my grandad every time Andy Gray scores.

My grandad walks me down to the bus station to see Johnny off on the coach. Johnny is meeting Carlo, his mate from work. All the supporters are hanging around waiting for the coach. There's a gold and black flag flying and a caravan selling bacon sandwiches. Everyone boos at a bloke that gets off the number 74 wearing a blue and white Albion scarf. He sticks his fingers up at us and we all cheer. In the corner of the bus station, down by the church, I see Steve and Paulie. They've got a sign: PHOTOS WITH THE WOLVES 50P. Next to the sign are two big cut-outs of John Richards and Andy Gray. People wander over and have their pictures taken standing next to the cut-outs, laughing.

They're using our camera.

Thass a good idea, ay it? My grandad nods towards Steve and Paulie. Dun yer want yer photo done, Sean?

I shake my head.

Am yer sure?

My grandad looks at me; he can't work me out.

The coach pulls up. Carlo arrives, takes a can of beer from a carrier bag and passes one to Johnny.

My grandad takes a few steps towards the sign for the photos and I think, he'll know, he'll notice. Then he stops suddenly and looks across at the Empire Tavern and down the slope again, but I see he's looking past Paul and Stevie, who are putting Andy Gray and John Richards into a bin bag, as people walk past us to get on the coach, some of them singing, Wemb-er-ley, Wemb-er-ley.

My grandad turns to me and says, Dyer know where I am?

I don't know what to say.

I was born right here, on this spot, he says. This was the back room in our house, right here.

He looks around like he has never thought about this before. There are clouds of blue exhaust coming from the coach. The castle is behind him. The house he lived in was knocked down years ago. My grandad has to step back onto the pavement as the coach starts to pull away.

We wave to Johnny and Carlo. Steve and Paulie have gone. My grandad takes me for a hot chocolate in Beatties where we're going to meet my mum.

Wolves won the cup. Andy Gray scored when Peter Shilton and David Needham collided, leaving him with an open goal, and they held on to the end. When we got back from town, we listened to it on the radio in the kitchen in Crow Street, me and Ronnie ran in and out through the back door and up and down the gardens in excitement when we scored. We had a good side that year, came sixth in the league; played in Europe the next season. We all went to the PSV Eindhoven game, the floodlights glowing and lighting up the green of the pitch and the old gold shirts. My grandad told me about Honved, how he'd been there, how Wolves had been the best in the world.

Again, it was my grandad who could see what was coming.

But where's this money from? he'd ask, and my dad and Johnny would shrug. A million pounds on a centre-forward here, a few million on a new stand there. Iss madness, he'd say.

Doh worry abaht it, Dad.

Stan Cullis day need millions of pounds.

All right.

And he had a team we'd stand in the rain to watch. We day need a fancy stand.

Yome living in the past, Dad. Iss the way of the world.

I can see that, and I can see what's coming.

He was right. The money wasn't there. They went down the next year, got bought out and came back up, then down again and again and again. The ground fell apart. The papers got the obituaries ready: receivership, bankruptcy, liquidation. That was the language of those days. They'd beaten Honved thirty years before that; they were the best side in the world then.

They should pack it up now, my grandad said when Johnny came in through the back door that time they lost to Chorley, part-timers.

They was unlucky, Johnny said.

Yer can say that again, son.

Thirty years or more is what you need, I think, if you really want to destroy something; community, society, whatever you want to call it. It takes a long time for things to die.

It's what you planned for, if there was a plan. After the first shocks, keep the pressure up. Sell off what you can, every last scrap. Maintain this permanent crisis; turn the world upside-down. You rob from the poor you've made and give to the rich. And you keep going, unrelenting. The revolution is permanent, after all.

Not everything dies, though. Some things linger on. The Wolves are still here, for one thing, resurrected. I take Joshua now and he loves it. *Fight, fight,* they sing, and *You'll never die, you'll never die,* to the tune of 'The Red Flag'.

Margaret Thatcher starts shooting people during the World Snooker final. We are all watching it at my nan and grandad's, Sunday afternoon going on Sunday night. Alex Higgins is our man. We love him. Everyone loves him. He plays fast and hits the balls hard. The other players stand and scratch their heads for ages and put chalk on their cues; Alex sniffs and jerks his head and knocks the balls around. Whenever I play snooker on the little table I got last Christmas I try and hit the ball on the side like Alex Higgins and send it swerving down the table. All the other players hit the white ball in the middle but Alex hits it on the side – check side or running side; one side or the other – and the balls thump into the pocket or creep in there gently and the white ball bounces and swerves off the cushions and Alex is ready for the next shot before the balls have stopped moving. Come on, Alex, we say when he gets a chance to win a frame; even my nan, who loves him too. He hits shots in the match where we gasp, all there in the front room, like the crowd at the Crucible, like when he pots the pink using the rest and knocks the black off the cushion and gets to ninety-three. It feels good, all of us sitting there together.

Then Margaret Thatcher starts shooting people.

One minute Alex is there, trying not to lose his concentration, which he always does at some point, it's his Achilles' heel; the next minute there's a picture of men standing, crouching, in the street with guns. Everyone talks at once so I can't hear the television. Next to the men dressed in black with guns is another man in a grey suit jacket rolling up a piece of carpet. It looks heavy. The men dressed in black point their guns at a row of white houses. The houses are big, with columns at the front and nice balconies. I imagine that they're the kind of house my dad plans for us to live in one day. The man with the grey jacket carries the heavy carpet along the front of the houses. Another man helps, carrying the back end. Something drops out of the side of the carpet and I see that it's an arm, a pale arm flopping around from inside the rolled up carpet. I realize that the flopping arm belongs to someone who is dead and although I saw my great-granny when she was dead, this is different, on television, someone who's been shot. I think, If I'd died when I fell out of the window this is how my dad and grandad would've carried me.

My mum says, Oh my God, Francis, and then everyone else realizes what the arm is. Harry Robertson is outside the window, looking at half a car that is leaning against the kerb, missing it all. I don't understand why he's not watching the snooker in the first place. Then my grandad leans forward and swears and changes sides on the telly and there's John Wayne in a film and everyone shouts at my grandad and he turns the channel back again. There are men, soldiers, dressed in black, standing on the balconies of the beautiful houses.

It's the SAS, my dad says. I can't tell from his face whether that's good or not.

Whose side am we on? I whisper to Johnny but he doesn't hear me.

Then there's an explosion, a bang and a flash of fire and a big cloud of smoke so you can't see the buildings any more, and there's a cloud of smoke drifting down the street. We all call out when the explosion comes, louder even than when Alex knocked the ball off the table when he was trying a mad shot. I can see the shape of Harry Robertson standing looking through the window at our television. The soldiers shoot; they fire their guns through the blasted windows, then they all jump through, into the buildings; then there is nothing, just the white buildings and the balconies and the reporter's voice talking.

The soldiers in black are the SAS. My dad explains who they are to my mum. I don't know who they are shooting. Iranian gunmen it says on the television. Flames jump out *of one of the windows; fire is coming from the broken windows.*

There has been a siege and hostages. I understand that bit. Hostages are when you keep someone prisoner. Six people are dead. It's a great success for the SAS, for Margaret Thatcher, the reporter says. At the Crucible, Alex loses concentration completely and loses the final 18–16. If Johnny really wants a revolution he'll have to fight against the SAS. But he couldn't even fight the skinheads.

Back at school there's no football for a day while we all play SAS because everyone's so excited about it. We get into trouble for being too violent. No one's dead, though, I want to say. People love them, the SAS, except me. I can see them in Crow Street, climbing on the rooftops and creeping down the entries, that one in the suit, the ones with guns and balaclavas, looming up outside the window of my nan and grandad's house, smashing their way inside, coming up out of the trees at the back of our house. They are coming. I know it. No one else seems to think so. They are coming, if we try to get rid of Margaret Thatcher, like the police banging on the front door or the plague of spiders coming for their revenge, that's for sure.

I started to go to the library on my own about then. My mum used to leave me there if she was shopping in Dudley; much later I'd walk down there on my own after school if nothing else was going on. When I'd read all the books I liked in the children's section, the Narnia books, *The Wind in the Willows*, Tom Sawyer and Huck Finn, Willard Price's adventure books, *Shakespeare for Children*, *Oliver Twist*, I would go and sit upstairs at the big table where the college students did their work, to read history books. I started with what we did at school, that was how I read so much about the Victorians, but once I'd started, one thing led to another. I used to carry an exercise book with me and write down anything interesting. I ended up with a pile of them that ran from when I was nine until I was fourteen, thirty or forty of them: my assassination diaries. I would think about the books on the shelves, the way the light moved around the reference library depending on what time of day it was, and all the knowledge inside the books, and I'd look at the growing pile of books in the corner of my room; in our house to start with and then, later, back at my nan and grandad's and the room I'd fallen out of.

I burned them later, my assassination diaries, out the back, in an oil drum, letting the wind take the smoke and ash out over the abandoned allotments. Burning books is where I ended up.

'And, you know, there is no such thing as society. There are individual men and women, and there are families. And no government can do anything except through people, and people must look to themselves first.'

That night my mum sits at the kitchen table and cries and my dad smashes his fist on the table three times. I get up from bed and listen from the stairs. I doh know what we'll do, my mum says.

I'll think of summat.

I just doh know what we'll do. I told yer, Francis.

Listen to me.

I day vote for em. So whatever happens yer cor blame me. My mum is crying really hard now but I can tell my dad isn't going to hit her or anything; he's standing at the kitchen table ready to thump it.

It ay nothing to do with that, my dad says and slams the table again and then he starts speaking slowly. I doh want yer to worry abaht any of it. It'll be fine, we'll be fine. If I lose me job I'll get another.

It ay as simple as that, Francis.

It is.

The next morning my dad takes me to the park to play tennis before he goes off to work, even though it's Sunday. When I get back I sit in the garden for a bit and watch a squirrel climb up the scaffolding for the new houses while the radio plays inside and my mum does some work in the kitchen and everything is okay.

I swear that bastard Eric has took the camera.

My grandad spent months rummaging in drawers for it, muttering to himself.

It ud be just the sort of trick he'd play. I knowed he was no good all along.

Every night after school Little Ronnie likes to walk over to the Ash Tree, find a stick from somewhere, and rattle the gates until Caesar, the big Alsatian, goes for us; howling and dribbling and jumping up at the gates. Sometimes the woman who keeps the pub leans out of the window to shout and we run off or flatten ourselves against the wall so she can't see us. I don't like doing it. I'm scared of the dog, that he'll get his jaws through the railings and bite us; or that instead of shouting from the window the woman will come down the steps and grab us, with her rollers in looking like Medusa, and she'll turn us into stone, or lock us in the cellar.

We look for planks of wood at the back of the row of old houses that the council hasn't finished pulling down. We're not meant to go near the empty houses. There are only a few left now; it's mostly piles of rubble. This is where the gypsies camped. Men have been working on it all summer. Paul Hill goes and plays in the houses, Jermaine did too, before he left. At school, they tell us not to go near the houses because they're dangerous.

Am yer allowed? Paul asks us. It's a stupid question. No one's allowed, not even adults. Even Charlie Clancey has to sneak in there in the middle of the night to see if there's any rag and bone.

I'm allowed, I say, but I doh want to.

I'm not allowed to go anywhere in the dark on my own, let alone the ruined houses to set off fireworks.

Paul makes chicken noises and runs around until Michelle says, Why would he want to go playing in them stupid houses wi yow? He's got better things to do. There's a spell on them houses, any road. Anyone who goes in there dies before they leave school. It's happened to loads of people. My nan told me. There's a ghost in there. It's an old woman who puts kids in a hole in the ground because all her own babbies died in a fire.

Paul shuts up for a bit but then asks if we want to go to the houses to see if we can see the ghost.

I say no thanks and then he says, No, too busy gooin off to the library.

He saw me one night after school. He was with his mum, they'd been to buy some shoes in the Arcade and they were coming out the entrance when I came walking up the road with a pile of books under my arm. Paul's mum made a big fuss of bumping into me and told him he should be like me getting books from the library to help with his school work and it was why I was clever and he kept getting bad reports. He looked shy when she was talking but the next day at school he started calling me the Librarian.

I know what I should do: tell him to fuck off or punch him or at least threaten to fight him, but I don't do anything. I feel like I did with the skinheads at the zoo. I look at him as he says it and then I look away and pretend he hasn't said anything at all and that I don't mind being called the Librarian.

At least he can read, Michelle says and looks like she might punch Paul herself. Then she goes, A-a-a, k-k-k, like Paul does when he's trying to read out loud and he goes red in the face.

Yer shunt let him call yer names, she says to me.

Ronnie likes to go to the ruined houses as well, even though he's not allowed out either. Sometimes he sneaks out with his older sisters and their boyfriends, especially when his mum's out, because his dad can't keep track of them all and goes out to mess with the cars in the street instead. His dad can't remember all their names, I swear. The other day in the street I asked whose birthday was next, because they always have a party, and he looked at Julie for a while and then said, That one.

Paul got taken home by the police one time, because they drove past when he was jumping out of an upstairs window of one of the old houses. It was nearly bonfire night and he'd been setting bangers off inside the empty rooms. I can't think of anything worse than being arrested. I'm not scared of the ghost, I know Michelle made that up, even though she swears it's true, but I am scared of the police.

Johnny tells me that the police are corrupt, which means they only do things for themselves, or for people who give them money or for the people who control them, like Margaret Thatcher. He tells me that they arrest loads of people who haven't even done any crime and tell them to say they have done it and then they beat them up. He says it happens all the time. It's one of the reasons there are so many problems. They keep beating you until you sign a confession. Johnny goes on a demonstration about it. Paul says the police were all right and took him on a ride round in the car before they drove him to his front door. When Johnny starts complaining about the police, my grandad says, Well, doh do nothing wrong, then.

Bonfire night was always this time of equal anticipation and dread. There'd be the smell of smoke and dead leaves all that week and the smoke would make a fog that wreathed the hills and muffled sounds, apart from the screaming of rockets down entries or the crack of bangers in abandoned houses.

I made a guy with Ronnie that year. We sat on the back step and stuffed a pair of Natalie's tights with screwed up newspaper. I imagined the tights on Natalie's legs and thought of the pictures in the drawer in Johnny's room. It was the only time we did a guy. We used to have a bonfire at my nan and grandad's but no guy, just fireworks, then we'd go to the big fire at Cinderheath on the Saturday. My nan didn't like the guy. Who could blame her really, when you think about it, everyone cheering the burning of a man?

We need a face, Ronnie says, sticking a paper plate on the deflated football we are using for a head.

Less just draw one, I say.

The one we'd seen at the top of Churchill Precinct, with older boys from the Rosland estate rattling a tin, had got a line drawn on for a mouth and two dots for eyes.

Yer doh atta mek him look handsome.

Lights are coming on along the row of houses and shreds of fog have settled across the allotments. There's a smell of dying leaves and smoke. It starts to rain. I want to get inside.

Here yam, boys. Why doh yer use this?

My grandad gets up from the kitchen table and comes to the back door. He rips a page from the newspaper: Margaret Thatcher's face. He laughs.

We fix her onto the football and then we burn her on the night; we cheer and bake potatoes in her embers.

We'd drive past Holbeche House occasionally. It would be a Sunday afternoon, summertime, with boards at the roadside advertising strawberry picking. Holbeche House was where the gunpowder plot ended. The plotters were all from the Midlands apart from Guy Fawkes himself, who was from York.

The plot's real leader was Robert Catesby; it was Catesby who should have been on the bonfire. I read about him in the library, the best sword fighter in England, a friend of Sir Walter Raleigh, and Shakespeare's cousin's cousin's cousin. I wrote about him in one of my notebooks. When we had our assembly at school about how the gunpowder plotters were caught, I knew I was on their side, that they were our men. It wasn't about religion, though. Apart from my nan, no one in my family was interested in that. My mum didn't want me to go to church school, would roll her eyes if my nan suggested it and say I was fine where I was. Anyway, I came to love Cromwell as much as Robert Catesby; more so, maybe, because he won, after all. It was the idea of rebellion that I liked, the sense of revolution; of a world turned upside-down.

When the plotters escaped to Holbeche House they were chased by the Sherriff of Worcester and his men. There was a siege. Robert Catesby mistakenly left gunpowder that had got wet out in front of the fire and it set light, injuring some of the plotters. As smoke poured from the windows of Holbeche House, the sheriff's soldiers started shooting and climbed in through the windows. Catesby was shot dead. The plotters who lived were taken to London to be tortured and killed.

Me and Ronnie get our sticks as usual, rattle the gates, and instead of feeling the vibrations come through my hand and then through my whole body, which is the best bit of the whole thing, the gate swings open and Caesar runs from his kennel. He comes right for us, teeth bared, like a wolf. I shut my eyes and wait to feel his jaws sink into my flesh or for him to crash me to the floor and then go for my throat. I can hear Ronnie wailing, standing next to me. Caesar's paws skitter on the concrete, I get a whiff of his breath and fur and he runs straight between us. I open my eyes as he sprints into the road, almost into a police car that slams to a halt, past a woman with a pram on the opposite pavement, into the rubble of the first row of demolished houses, before he jumps through the glass-less window of the old butcher's shop. We hear him howling across the wasteland.

Come on, I say. I grab Ronnie's arm and try to run. The woman with the pram is staring at us but the police haven't got out of their car yet and the woman who keeps the pub hasn't arrived at the window. If we can get to the church we can run through the graveyard, out into the field where they buried the cholera dead, over the main road, into the allotments and in through the back door of the Robertsons' and into Ronnie and his sisters' bedroom in about two minutes. Even if the police come round after us one of his sisters could say she'd walked home from school with us.

The pub doors fly open and the woman stands there in her curlers and dressing gown and shouts, Get here!

She's shouting at us. There's no sign of Caesar. We've still got the planks of wood in our hands. The police car passenger door opens and a policewoman gets out to the crackle of the radio.

I cor move, says Ronnie, as I shuffle towards the pub.

Get here, now! the woman shouts again, which gets Ronnie started, his head bowed.

We get to the pub steps together: Ronnie, me and the policewoman. The policeman pulls the car into the kerb. He even flashes the lights and puts the siren on for a second. I want to drop the wood, but I can't seem to let go.

This has been gooin on for months an I've had enough of these bleedin kids pestering my dog. The woman's voice booms along the road even though we are all standing right next to each other now. The policeman joins us as well. They're both holding their hats in their hands like someone's died. I look at the handcuffs and truncheons on their belts and think I'm going to be sick.

Months of torment, mekkin that dog's life a misery. She is laying it on a bit strong now. I think Caesar quite enjoys our visits. I reckon he waits for us to have a good bark and jump up at the gates. We give him an excuse. I'm the one who doesn't like it. Ronnie starts to cry.

No use bleartin now, yer little bully, the woman goes on.

The police haven't said anything yet.

I look out across the hill from the steps. There's a street of rubble where they knocked the old houses down, piles of old bricks with rags and bits of pipe sticking out of them, then the row of empty houses, with the boards pulled back from the windows and doors so kids like Paul can play there, and Charlie Clancey can get in to take the copper pipes before the council get them. Beyond the rubble is our school and then the top of the hill. I can see Rodney James doing keep-ups on the football pitch, waiting for the others to come out I suppose. Lorries are rumbling past on the main road. There's the streak of rain from a

*cloud somewhere over the hill. I wonder where it's falling
and wish that I was there instead of here.*

Cromwell killed the king. I had a bag of model roundheads
and cavaliers. They fought a real war, not like at Holbeche
House or at the Iranian Embassy, but one with proper
battles. I would put the cavaliers in the castle and the
roundheads would surround it and then there'd be a siege.
At some point the roundheads would come and knock
the castle down. That was pretty much what happened in
the actual war. Cromwell Green was named after Oliver
Cromwell; Kates Hill after one of his men. Before that
Kates Hill had been called Cawney Hill, after the crows
and ravens and old English birds. Cromwell won: there'd
been a revolution. He called England the Commonwealth
and called himself the Lord Protector. When you win you
get to give places new names: Londonderry, the Falkland
Islands, Bombay. That's another of the reasons I changed
the name of the pub, because I could, because I'd won.

It's strange, though, you hear different stories over time.
Since we were told all that at school, I've heard that Kates
Hill was first called Cats Hill, from the days when they'd
clear the castle and the market of wild cats, put them all
on a wagon and release them on the hill, which didn't have
a name then and was woods where no one lived except
witches. And that Cawney Bank wasn't named after the
crows at all, but after the rabbits, coneys, that burrowed
into its side. Perhaps the truth doesn't matter in the end;
it's only the stories that count.

*A shape comes from the entry at the side of the butcher's
shop. I used to wait there with my nan when I was in*

the infants school, for pork chops and tomato sausage and caul, when she made faggots. There was a tiled floor and the sun would come through the window and make the knives shiny; there was a calendar on the wall with pictures of cows in green, sunny fields. The room would feel hot and smell of blood. Now my nan goes down to Cinderheath or Shakespeare's on Watson's Green Road. When the shape comes from the shadows of the entry, you can see it's a man, limping, holding a dog on a rope.

Caesar! the woman shouts now and looks across the road. Here he is, padding through the rubble, a piece of old rope round his neck as a lead, being walked along by Tommy Clancey who has a can of beer in his other hand and an unlit cigar in his mouth. It turns out that he's been living in the abandoned flat above the old butcher's for weeks. Tommy and Caesar zigzag through the piles of bricks to the sign that says DANGER, where Caesar cocks his leg, and Tommy, swapping the lead to his beer hand undoes his zip and goes as well, splattering the base of the sign. When they finish, Tommy strolls out on to the pavement, looks both ways very carefully, and comes across the road with a panting Caesar.

We get taken home in the police car. Well, to Ronnie's first. I say that I live next door, at my nan and grandad's. Paul is lying about the police being all right. They tell us that if the dog had been hurt we'd have had to go to court and probably get sent away to juvenile detention. Then they make a big show of knocking on Ronnie's front door first and then my nan and grandad's. There's only my nan in. She has to phone my mum. My nan is never angry with me but today her face goes white with *rage. She has to ask the police in while they wait for my mum to come. They come in through the front door. She makes them a cup of tea. I sit on a chair staring at the floor. Then when my mum comes, we get the big lecture all over again. I can hear Ronnie getting a good hiding next door. It's probably what they do if they take you in for questioning, beat someone up in the cell next door to scare you. The police tell my mum about all the trouble they've had with kids causing problems with the houses. My mum is good, though. She says I've never been allowed anywhere near that site and if the council or the builders put a proper fence up around it to make it safe then maybe there wouldn't be as many problems. The police want to go after that. The policeman keeps eyeballing me, like he wants to hit me with his truncheon. I feel bad for Caesar. It would have been terrible if he'd got lost or run over or something but we hadn't meant for him to escape. It was a game.*

The police talk quietly again to my mum as she lets them out of the front door. When they've gone she comes back in and pounds me round the head and tells me to get out of her sight. I go upstairs and sit on the edge of the toilet seat and don't dare move for a while. I have never been in so much trouble. I haven't even had chance to say that we found Tommy Clancey.

He'd been sleeping in the old butcher's shop since he returned from Stourport. That was how he lived, heading out to the countryside towns for the summer: Bridgnorth, Bewdley, Stourport. He'd sleep out by the river and then head back to Dudley for the winter, picking up work as he went. He lived like that for years. He was still doing it when I came back for good. The woman who kept the pub, Diane, was so grateful to him for bringing Caesar back that she lifted his ban, which meant that he was banned from every pub in Dudley apart from the Ash Tree. He even did a bit of work collecting glasses and changing the odd barrel. She paid him in drink. Caesar carried on into old age, barking at children as they walked past the gates.

Nearly an hour, they was sitting in here, my nan says. Nearly an hour. Longer than when they come last time. They could've been off catching crooks. Instead, they was drinking tea in here and walking the mud off their boots onto the clean hall carpet.

She doesn't say this to me, but to my mum.

I know, Mum, I know.

They want to be ashamed of theerselves. I day like the look of him, the policeman, looking at Sean like he was a criminal.

I know, Mum, I know.

All children get into devilment every now and again.

I know, but he shouldn't have done it.

I blame them next door. They want to get that Little Ronnie to behave.

We can hear his shouts through the wall.

No good tanning him now, my nan continues. They should've given him some discipline before.

No, but Sean is responsible for his own behaviour, Mum.

They should be more worried about that dog biting somebody, I doh know about the kids playing with it. I can see why yer want to move. Away from all this carry-on.

Okay, it's done with now. Let's see what happens about moving. It's nothing to do with this.

My mum doesn't speak to me for days. When she does, all she says is that I shouldn't have said to the police to take me to my nan and grandad's. That makes me feel even worse because I thought I'd done the right thing. We were going to Ronnie's anyway and I thought my mum would worry about a police car in our street. I'm banned from seeing Ronnie for a week. I think it's going to be worse again when my dad comes in, but he just says to never do it again and falls asleep in the chair during Coronation Street.

The next day me and Ronnie tell Paul about what happened and he doesn't believe us.

Diane kept the pub for twenty years or more. Her husband had walked out not long after they'd taken it on, didn't like the hours, went off with a woman from Langley Green. Tommy would come back every now and again, like he did. Diane gave me my first proper pub job when I turned eighteen. She didn't remember who I was. I told her one Saturday night when we stayed for a lock-in. She laughed. I worked weekends; learned the cellar in the week. Caesar had replacements over the years. There was a Doberman called Brutus when I worked there. Diane lives with her sister in Tenerife now. The pub's boarded up. Kids break in and cause mischief. Everything worth nicking from it has gone. I had a look at buying it, but there's no saving the place. They'll knock it down soon.

Sunday mornings my dad takes me for a walk down the canal, if he's not at work. There are abandoned buildings where the first workshops and factories were. Cobb's Engine House is near the start of the tunnel that goes under the hill and comes out in Tipton. It used to pump all the water out of the mines. Johnny wanted to paint a picture of it. Henry Ford, who made the cars, bought the engine to put it in a museum in America. People go to the ruin to sniff glue now, older boys, young men, punks, skinheads; it says NF all over the walls.

One Sunday morning, we see some skinheads on the path ahead of us and I realize that Steve, Paulie and Yvette are there, part of this group of ten, fifteen, shaved heads with bottles and bags stood in front of the engine house and the ridges of long grass, blocking the path. I think about how Johnny said there were thirty of them, how he knocked one in the cut, how he fought them. I know now that he didn't fight them.

I want us to cut across the grass and head down to the canal towpath that way but my dad walks a few steps in front and I know he won't move for anyone.

Come on, woss the matter? he says and I shuffle along and look down at the path like when Johnny looked down at the concrete at the zoo.

The skinheads won't move. I can see that. There's Steve and Paulie standing right in the middle of the path with a few others. Yvette is patting a dog, a grey whippet that another girl skinhead is holding on a lead. I like whippets. My grandad has taken me down to the Mushroom Field in Cromwell Green where they race whippets on summer nights and the men stand around and bet with each other and count out money into one another's hands. We saw Charlie Clancey race his dog, Angel, and he came over and spoke to us. He looked angry because his dog was slow. Angel had hard, gleaming eyes like the dog on the path now.

Angel's a devil, Charlie had said, making himself laugh.

They still haven't moved and my dad is walking more quickly, I swear, right at them. I drop back. He says, Come on, Sean, but doesn't turn his head to look at me; he's staring at Steve and Paulie and the other skinheads now. One of them is taller and thinner than Steve and Paulie and has a swastika tattooed on his neck. I can see it clearly because we're so close to them. They've stopped talking to each other and are looking at my dad. He doesn't slow down.

All right, he says quietly, a few steps away from Steve and the one with the swastika who looks, and looks, and then steps off the side of the path so my dad can walk right between them.

All right, mate, Steve mumbles, and I notice that he looks down as my dad passes. My dad doesn't even look at him.

Hello, Sean, Yvette says and looks up from the dog with a smile, All right?

All right. I nod, nearly running after my dad now.

Iss Sean look, Paulie says. I can tell he's drunk or whatever because of how bright his eyes are. There's a bag of glue rustling in his hand. He puts his thumb up. I put mine up to him too. My dad turns briefly and I hurry to keep up with him.

Who's yer mates? he asks with half a smile.

Oh, Johnny knows em, I say.

He motions down to the towpath and the mouth of the tunnel and we carry on with our walk like nothing's happened.

My dad showed me where the canals went and how they joined up. Where we sat, where it was flat and broad, the horses used to pull the barges along but up ahead, my dad pointed, in the tunnel, men had to lie on their backs and leg the boat along through the darkness. I said I would've liked to do that and he smiled and said how much hard work it would be. But that was good; work was good. The canals met the river at Stourport. The river flows out through Worcester and then on to the sea, other rivers joining it as it goes, into the Bristol Channel and the Irish Sea and then the cold, dark Atlantic. I remember realizing how everything was connected, pictured supertankers, Spanish galleons, nuclear submarines, sailing up the viscous water of the cut from all the strange places in the world; Matsuyama, Paramaribo, Archangel, places I'd look at in the atlas on the big table upstairs in the library.

The skinheads couldn't knock us off the path. It was them that had to step out of the way for us. My place was secure in the world, right here, settled, and I remember a feeling of peace. I could hear the shouts from the football pitches over the hill and the skinheads laughing and smashing bottles, but they were nothing to us now. I remember the feeling of warmth and safety, like the feeling when I sat round at my nan and grandad's with the fire on in the winter before everyone started to bang on the door and come in for Sunday tea.

I understood that the place where we lived was old, ancient. There were stories and secrets running through it. The ground beneath our feet was nine-tenths hollow, dug out for limestone. We were held up by insect skeletons millions of years old. There had once been a tropical sea where we lived now. I read how the top of the hills that we lived on had once been the bottom of the sea. I collected trilobites in a Quality Street tin. Ronnie's dad took us to Wren's Nest to find some and we went to Saint Francis's to see the windows and down to the cemetery to put flowers on Duncan Edwards' grave.

What'll we do if there's a war?

Head to the caves, son. We'd all live underground, my grandad says.

I can see that, when I ask, my mum is worried because she doesn't know the answer. She hasn't been in a war like my grandad. He knows what to do. Margaret Thatcher might start a war to help her new friend, Ronald Reagan, who is the new President of the United States of America.

Fool, him, my grandad says, as he watches Ronald Reagan on the television. They'd have bin better off with the monkey.

Ronald Reagan used to act in films with a chimpanzee called Bonzo.

The television shows Russian tanks rumbling through Moscow and the soldiers marching along with big steps and boots, then the screen switches to Ronald Reagan smiling and waving, back in America. I like to watch the Russian soldiers march when they show it on television on May Day. May Day is workers' day, so the Russian soldiers march for us under their red flags and hammers and sickles. The people's flag is deepest red. It's complicated, though, because the Russian soldiers still might come and kill us even though they'd be attacking Margaret Thatcher and we'd have to try to make friends with them, our enemy's enemy.

If there's a war the Russians will drop a nuclear bomb on Birmingham, so we'd have to go underground and live in the caves. That's how human life might survive. When I look at the patterns of the trilobites' bodies I think of the labyrinth underneath us, the twists and turns. There are lakes and great caverns under Dudley. There's one by the zoo called the Singing Cavern that's so big you'd have to ride across it in a ship. That's where we'll live when they drop their bombs.

I used to dream of Theseus striding through the labyrinth to kill the minotaur, of Bilbo creeping through the misty mountain tunnels with his magic ring, stories from the books I read. I imagined how we'd evolve as we lived underground, how we'd end up with huge eyes and curved backs like the Morlocks in *The Time Machine.* Slowly we'd change into pale frogs, worms, burrowing back into the water and the dark.

Sean said hello to some of yower mates this morning, day yer, Sean?

As my dad says this I see Johnny flinch at the kitchen table and I don't want my dad to say anything more.

Day yer, Sean? my dad says again because I'm ignoring him. I nod.

Oh, right, Johnny says.

My dad is smiling. He thinks it's funny that I might know the skinheads. I'm not sure why. He must know they're not Johnny's mates, could never be.

Who was they, Sean? What was theer names?

I doh know, I say.

Well, they knowed yowers. Put their thumbs up.

I pretend I'm trying to remember. There's no point pretending. I could tell from Johnny's face that he knew who it was.

Is it Steve? I say. And Paulie and Yvette. They had a dog, a whippet.

Oh, right, Johnny says.

They looked well, my dad says. Skinheads. Wenches an all, with their hair shaved off. He says this as my grandad comes in the room.

What, them skinheads? Yow stay away from them. Doh get mixed up wi them. My grandad points the potato peeler at Johnny. He has been peeling potatoes for my nan. And doh get him mixed up wi em. We want yow to keep yer hair on, doh we, Sean, eh?

All right, they ay really me mates, Johnny says.

Doh get mixed up wi em, I'm telling yer. My grandad keeps the potato peeler aimed at him.

All right, Johnny says. I am twenty years old, though. Iss up to me who me mates am.

I'm tellin yer. My grandad keeps staring at him.

Later, Johnny talks to my dad quietly at the kitchen table. He keeps looking up to check my grandad isn't listening. My dad nods his head then he gets up to pour a drink and pats Johnny on the shoulder, tells him not to worry about it.

They were beautiful; Johnny's drawings, paintings. He'd draw all the time, in soft pencil in the first place, in the sketchbooks he kept on the go: cobwebs, the castle, the line of factory roofs. He didn't do people very often, apart from those pictures of Natalie, and the portrait he did of my mum. On Sundays or on light nights when he was back from work in time he'd do watercolours, flowers or the shed, a row of cabbages over the fence in the allotments, the clouds floating over us. At the caravan he'd sit with his back to the sea wall and paint green-black seaweed and orange starfish or the light falling on the hills.

He tried to show me sometimes. We'd sit together at the kitchen table and I'd try to copy the lines he made on the page but I couldn't even do that. It was about a way of looking at things. I had my books. I could see things in my own head. I thought about how he looked at things, though, tried to see some of the magic.

I think of them now, Johnny's drawings, with the cable-cars moving in an arc across the town, cobwebs threading between geraniums. He still draws, I know that. There are piles of sketchbooks in the corner of his bedroom. The rest are in the loft. I never ask him about it. I did once, when we first started doing food. I asked him about putting some up, seeing if people would buy them. He nodded and said yes, but didn't offer anything. I think of Jermaine's face when I asked him that time and his son, yeah, piss artist, and I think of the pile of exercise books I used to have, up in smoke, the plans for an assassination, a revolution. I'm glad they're ash. Whereas, Johnny's sketchbooks: I should ask him again.

About the time I went to work for Diane, the Richardson brothers published plans to build the world's tallest tower at Merry Hill, next to the new shopping centre. We could have looked out to sea from the top. Each day, the pub would have been in its shadow for a while. It was ridiculous, but by that point anything was possible. It never got built, but the idea itself was enough. I've put copies of the drawings up in an alcove by the bar and Lubetkin's animal houses up over where the old fireplace was. I'd like Johnny's cable-cars up there, somewhere, his cobwebs too, if only I could ask him properly.

The Sunday after that walk with my dad, he and Johnny went out together. That afternoon the camera was sitting on the kitchen table.

I knew it'd turn up eventually, my grandad said.

I found it at the back of the cupboard, Johnny said.

Johnny took me to the park one night that week and we saw Steve walking down Watson's Green Road towards us. He had a black eye, crossed the road when he saw us coming.

You should fight fire with fire.

Yvette, Steve's old girlfriend, comes in the pub sometimes with her husband. She works at an old people's home in Blackheath. She worked for a while with Michelle at the day centre; Michelle says she's a lovely woman. Yvette's hair is permed now.

Kids all right? she asks. They am gerrin big. I doh know where the time gos, Sean, I doh.

People lived in the caves until the fifties, not underground, but in the rock houses down at Kinver Edge. The Edge is what's left of a desert, millions of years old. We'd visit sometimes on quiet afternoons, and me and Ronnie would scramble up and down in the forest, climbing the cliff and the trees, our hands red with sandstone. There were ashes in some of the caves from recent fires, shapes cut into the walls for what had been shelves, graffiti scored into the soft stone. This is where we'll live, I thought, as we ran up and down, pretending to be Robin Hood; this is where we'll come to disappear.

My mum cries at the kitchen table. John Lennon has been shot. He was in The Beatles. My mum sings their songs to me sometimes. She sits at the kitchen table crying. I'm not sure if it's only John Lennon she's crying about. I heard the door slam this morning in the pitch black, my dad off to work. Usually he's really quiet. Sometimes he even lets the handbrake off the car and rolls down the slope of the drive before he starts the engine along the street but this morning there was loads of noise, shouting, but I couldn't hear what they were saying apart from my mum hissing, Well, you do that then.

Don't cry, Mum, I say.

It's very sad, sweetheart.

Don't cry, Mum, I say, don't cry, and I realize when I say it that it does no good, even though she turns and gives me a hug and goes to warm up some milk in the saucepan for me to have on my Weetabix because it's cold outside. She has red eyes from crying when I get back that night and John Lennon is still playing on the radio and my dad is still at work.

While she's mashing potatoes my mum goes and gets a bottle of gin from the cupboard. She pours a glass and tips some of my orange squash into it. She doesn't normally do this. In fact, when they all have a drink on a Sunday, my mum has Britvic juice. That's not a drink. When you say you have a drink it means beer or wine or whisky or another drink you get in a pub. Sometimes my dad will let me have a sip of his beer or pour some in a glass with lemonade for shandy. I want to say something to her, as she looks at the glass and takes a big drink of it and then pulls a face. I want to make things better, but I can't think what to say and so she pours some more gin and squash.

All right, darling, come and have this while it's hot, and she puts my sausages and mash on the table. She smiles. I can't do anything about John Lennon getting shot. I can't do anything to make my dad come back from work. I can't do anything about my mum being sad.

It's not an excuse. What happened to my mum in the end, I could have done more, I could. Worse than that, I was part of the cause. That was the start of it, then. I can't blame Margaret Thatcher for that, for my own failure; though I did, I still do.

Christmas morning and my mum and dad are happy. I've got a tape recorder and a Subbuteo set. When we get to my nan and grandad's, everyone's smiling and laughing. They give me Wolves and Villa teams and I lay the pitch and the players out in the front room. I start a league: Wolves, Villa, Liverpool, Ipswich. When Ronnie comes back from visiting his nan and grandad in Kidderminster we'll play the FA Cup. He wants Man United as one of his presents. His dad, Natalie and the baby have stayed at home, next door.

Why ay yer all gooin, Ronnie? my nan asks him.

There ay no room in Kidderminster.

No room at the inn. My nan laughs.

I hear her whispering about it later with my mum.

It ay right, though, is it? Splitting a family up at Christmas.

Ronnie says he doesn't mind, he'll be back in a few days. It's like having two Christmases.

A poor clearance from George Berry . . . unusual for him . . . lets in Souness . . . Souness inside to Sammy Lee . . . nudged on to Dalglish . . . turns . . . Oh, what a goal! Dalglish into the far corner. Bradshaw had no chance there. Three–one to Liverpool, there doesn't look any way back for Wolves now. They will need to find some form for when they play Man United in the cup in the new year.

I am really fair and don't let the Wolves win and I record the commentaries on my new tape recorder and make a programme called Soccer Special. I discuss the big cup game, Wolves against Manchester United, in between the commentaries, so I can play it to Ronnie when he gets back. Johnny is drunk and comes on the programme to be interviewed. He pretends to be Brian Clough.

Now, listen, young man, he says, the only teams in red worth talking about are Nottingham Forest and the Soviet Union, no more talk of Liverpool and Manchester United, please.

I'm allowed to stay up on New Year's Eve and wait for midnight. We open the front door to let the New Year in and to shake hands with Harry, who feeds Natalie's baby with a bottle and staggers drunk up the entry. We open the back door to let the old year out. It is black and silent across the allotments and all the works. My grandad shivers and pours himself and my dad another whisky when we go back into the kitchen. Johnny is back from the pub and fetches a glass from the cupboard.

Happy New Year, he says.

Yow've had enough, son.

Yer doh know how much I've had.

I can tell the way yome looking at me.

I ay had no more than yow.

I said yow've had enough.

My grandad screws the top back on the whisky and puts it on the table. He wears a gold paper crown that has slipped almost over his eyes. He looks out at Johnny from underneath his crown until Johnny looks away. They both fall asleep in the chairs. Johnny wakes up after a few minutes and walks over to the table and pours himself a *glass of whisky and tops my dad up. I am meant to be in bed, asleep.*

The Wolves: if I'd known what was going to happen to them I'd have let them win everything while they could.

Later, people would ask if I was related to Steve Bull when they saw my name. At first I'd say no. We're not, as far as I know. Then I started mumbling some answer about him maybe being my cousin's cousin's cousin. Maybe he is. It was a useful thing to say when I bought the pub and was serving behind the bar. There are pictures of him up at either end of the bar; one of him banging a goal in for Wolves, one when he came on and scored for England against Scotland. He came in once; we got him to sign the pictures. There's a photo of him with Johnny and Josh pinned up next to the optics. The camera that my dad got back for us sits behind the till. I found it again, tucked in a drawer, bought some of the old film off the internet.

Ronnie isn't coming back. His dad sits at the kitchen table, talking to my nan. None of them are coming back. Ronnie's mum has left with a man who sells beer for the brewery. They weren't even in Kidderminster. The man is moving to a new job on the south coast, miles away, past London, and they are all going with him, Ronnie and his sisters and his mum. They are never coming back. My nan tells me to go upstairs while she talks to Harry. She puts a cup of tea down for him. My grandad tips some whisky into it.

Natalie stayed with her dad and the baby, Leah. Natalie never saw her mum again, couldn't forgive her. Leah died ten years ago, just before her twenty-first birthday. They found her in one of the boarded up houses on Cromwell Green; heroin.

Ronnie and I never got to play the Man United game. In the little ground I'd made around the Subbuteo pitch I'd done a board saying NEXT FIXTURE: MANCHESTER UNITED FA CUP. I left it there for ages; it made me think of the clock at Old Trafford that's stopped at the time of the Munich crash. I got a postcard from Ronnie once, from Brighton, where they'd go on day trips from the little town where they lived. Ronnie couldn't write that well but he said everything was okay and that he liked living by the sea, but he missed all of us, and Dudley. I wrote a long letter to him, but never got anything back. They moved around a lot. The brewery rep left them and Vanessa moved on to someone else.

I'd have her back, Lil, course I would, like a shot, tomorrow, I hear Harry say to my nan, sitting at the kitchen table. I'm trying to feed Albert the tortoise some lettuce through the fence. I can't get him to eat like Ronnie could. He used to pretend to talk to him in a tortoise language.

I doh think her's coming back, Ron.

I miss the kids. I miss her, he says. He's crying, a big man crying, and he isn't even drunk. My nan is standing up rubbing his back.

What am I gonna do, Lily? he says.

Iss all right, Harry, come on, my nan says. Come on, iss all right.

'Oh, but you know, you
do not achieve anything
without trouble, ever.'

A man shoots Ronald Reagan. He walks up to him and shoots. Bang, bang, bang, and the bodyguards jump on the man with the gun and on Ronald Reagan. I wonder if the man's a Russian agent. They show it on the news. Ronald Reagan doesn't die, though.

Iss like bloody voodoo, Johnny says when he sees it, and then the newsreader comes on to say that Ronald Reagan is fine and can carry on being president. I think Johnny thinks it would have been better if he'd been killed.

I know what voodoo is. There is a country called Haiti, where there is a ruler called Baby Doc Duvalier. His dad's name was Papa Doc Duvalier. I saw a picture in the Daily Mirror and a clip on the news. The people in Haiti are poor and miserable but they can't get rid of Baby Doc, or Papa Doc before him, because the Duvaliers have got their own police, like the SAS, called the Tonton Macoute and they have magical voodoo powers, because Baby Doc made a deal with the devil. This means that you can try to kill Baby Doc but he won't die. He'll probably rule Haiti for ever and the people will stay poor and miserable and frightened for ever unless someone can undo the magic. You can't undo it by shooting Baby Doc.

My grandad is angry all the time now. He is angry at the telly and even angrier at Johnny. My mum and dad are angry too, but only at each other.

There are riots in London, in Brixton. All the black men run around smashing windows and looting and throwing petrol bombs. A riot is when a group of you get together and go wild. Looting is when you take things that you might want but can't afford, like a new television set, from out of a shop after you've had the riot. A petrol bomb is a milk bottle with petrol in and a rag dipped in it and sticking out of the top. You set light to the rag and then throw it at the police. Johnny tells me how to make them. He laughs as the black men throw the bricks and petrol bombs at the police in Brixton. My grandad is angry with them and with Johnny.

They'm fighting back, Dad.

Fighting back at what?

This government. Yow ought to be grateful that somebody's got the spine to say enough's enough.

They ay fighting the government. They doh know who's in the government. They just wanna go wild and tek things that ay theers.

Well, have yer thought they might wanna take things cos they look around and see that other people have got things and they see how unfair it is? Yow've said yerself iss unfair. Yer tode me how unfair it is. From each according to his ability to each according to his need. Yow taught me that.

Here yam then, my grandad says, waving the newspaper apart in front of his face. Here yam. David Banks, sentenced to two years, receipt of stolen goods. The Woodhouses and the Bankses, they'm the people fighting our corner? I doh think so. Fightin their own corner. Givin everybody else a bad name.

The Woodhouses, some of Ronnie's uncles, and the Banks families are the two names you always hear to do with crime round by us. They are 'notorious criminal families' it says in the paper when they have the trial about robbing the post office.

It ay the same.

What dyer mean it ay the same? Crime's crime. This ay political.

Yow sound like bloody her now.

He means Margaret Thatcher.

I doh sound like nobody. Iss plain hooliganism. They ay political. Or if it is political, it ay nothing to do with my politics. The politics of I'll just take what I want even if doh belong to me, is what it is. The politics of I've never done a day's work in me life an I doh intend to if I can get away with thieving off everybody else. They got more in common with the Tories than wi me.

Yow ay mekkin sense now.

They should arrest em. And deport em.

What?

If they doh like it they can leave.

What dyer mean?

Well, if they've come from somewhere else then they can allus goo back theer.

I've heard it all now.

I mean it. They come here but it must be better than Jamaica or wherever because they've come here in the fust place. I know they've got it hard. Course they've got it hard, but it just meks it wuss for everybody else, rampaging around and not respecting the law. They'm theer *own wust enemies. They am. Yer see it round here. It ay right. It ay. Yow cor tell me iss right. That policeman who got injured, he's got a wife and family. They'll bloody kill somebody next and then where ull we be?*

Have you heard this? Johnny's eyes have gone wide and he's waving his arm towards my mum. He sounds like Enoch Powell.

There's no need for that, Dad. It doh matter what colour they am. My mum usually doesn't take sides. Usually she thinks what Johnny says is stupid. She looks angry with my grandad. He doesn't care, though.

Well, if thass true how come they'm all black? I doh see em rioting in Neath or Newcastle or rahnd here for that matter.

Yow wait, Johnny mutters.

Yer need to calm down, all on yer, my nan says. And doh start ropin her into yer argument, she says, pointing at my mum. Her's a married woman with a son. Her's got her own problems. Yer'd think we'd got enough to worry abaht without all this carry-on a hundred miles away. Let em riot if they want. It ay nothing to do with we.

Look, my grandad says slowly, putting the newspaper down on the table and his hand on Johnny's arm. All I'm saying is that they'm doin more harm than good. If yome serious about gerrin rid of the government then, yeah, protest, demonstrate all yer want, but yer doh have to break the law, tek other people's stuff, hurt people, not like that. There's a proper process. We have elections. If yer doh like the government then yer can vote to get rid of em. Thass how we do things.

And a fine mess thass got us in.

My grandad shrugs.

What if yome outside the process?

What dyer mean?

Well, if yer cor see that there's anybody representing your voice.

This is the blacks now, is it?

Well, yeah.

Well, tek Solomon Abrahams at our work, he voted Tory.

Thass it then, now. On the strength of one black man, they'm all Tories.

No, I ay sayin that. All I'm sayin is they've got a right to vote, same as anybody else. Solomon's a fool if he thinks voting Tory's gonna do him any favours but he's got every right to do so. I bet none of them voted. I bet none of them doing the rioting am even registered to vote.

Thass my point.

No, thass my point. They ay got a leg to stand on. Black, white, pink with yeller spots. They ay doin nobody any favours except theerselves. They should round em all up.

This tops the lot, this does.

They ay rioting to cause a revolution, son, they'm rioting so they can nick some tellies!

Right, thass it, yome finishing it now. I doh want to hear no more about it. No more, no more, no more.

My nan bangs the kitchen table each time she says No more. My grandad and uncle look shocked.

'Crime is crime
is crime, it is not
political.'

They had the same argument on and off for years. Later, during the miners' strike, when the miners fought the police at Orgreave, exactly one year after my dad died, I watched, excited, as they looked like they were winning. Arthur Scargill was arrested. You saw him being dragged off towards a police van still talking at the camera, wearing a cap with a slogan that you couldn't read. I wanted the miners to smash them.

Why doh they have a proper vote? my grandad had said.

They doh need one, Dad. We'm past that point.

Why have they all gotta come out, why not be strategic, tactical?

Her's gonna shut all the mines, Dad. Her's gonna close em all. Her's gonna close everything. Look around yer. Look what her's done here and we just rolled over. They've gorra fight. Iss now or never.

Why doh he listen to Kinnock?

Neil Kinnock wanted the miners to ballot before going on strike. Scargill said no. I could see what voting gave you. Voting gave you Margaret Thatcher. The more they attacked Scargill, the more I loved him.

I doh know why he doh have a vote, my grandad said, but that didn't stop him stuffing a few notes into the collection bucket that the miners brought to the marketplace in Dudley. I was with him. That money was for the gas bill, though. We'd seen one of my uncle Eric's new work vans drive past and it had sent my grandad into a rage. He held the money up to show him it was notes he was putting in there. The papers said the money came from Russia, from Libya, as well as from our gas bill. I wanted the miners to have guns. Arthur Scargill, too. They could get guns, weapons, all sorts. They could blow up police stations, power lines, the enemy. They needed to do more than throw a few rocks, I could see that. They might have been winning the fighting at Orgreave on the telly, but it was chaos and the next time the police would win. It was the same with the riots. Everyone would fight the police for a bit and smash windows and steal a few televisions, but then a few days later the police would be back in charge again.

You still hear people say Enoch was right. I've heard it muttered like a kind of mantra in the pub when I'm serving the last old men their pints of mild, when they're talking about whatever the latest disaster to plague the town is. People have been saying it pretty much since he made that speech, as an act of defiance, as a self-fulfilling prophecy. Two of them, Stan and Malcolm, were draymen back when there was the brewery walk-out in Wolverhampton in support of Powell, not long after the speech. They get the bus up from Gornal on a Saturday, sleeveless pullovers under their suits. They talk about how they stopped the traffic, how people looked at them, about how they were somebody. I don't say anything, serve the beer meekly and wipe the bar over and they sit there in their comfy chairs, drinking on the banks of the rivers of blood.

'I learned from childhood the dignity which comes from work and, by contrast, the affront to self-esteem which comes from enforced idleness. For us, work was the only way of life we knew, and we were brought up to believe that it was not only a necessity but a virtue.'

I hardly see my dad now. He's at work all the time. Machines break down and he has to fix them. That's his job. He goes to work at the normal time, half past six, and I hear him talking quietly to my mum while she makes him a cup of tea and then he'll be back late, or early, to have a sandwich and then go back out to work again. My mum is angry, I know that, at him going out to work, at the machines for always breaking down, at the men at the factory for always phoning up and asking if they can speak to Francis and can he come and fix the machine so they can cut more shapes in the steel and not lose their jobs. If you lose your job it means you can't go to work any more because the factory has to close down because the machines keep breaking or Margaret Thatcher doesn't want you to work there any more. It's happening all over the place. Even at Cinderheath, my grandad says, some of the men have been told not to come back. They've been made redundant. That means you have to sit around or stand on the step of your house drinking cups of tea not doing much. Instead of going to work you get given dole money by Margaret Thatcher. That sounds okay; being given money to listen to the radio and drink tea but it's no good. It isn't very much money, not if you worked in a factory and got paid your wages and did overtime and got

*paid time and a half for that as well. If you do that you are
rich, but if you get dole money you aren't rich any more.*

*Margaret Thatcher wants to stop our people being rich
and wants other people, her friends, to be rich. She's
attacking us because we rich and powerful and she doesn't
want us to be. I think she's jealous of us.*

*Do you think Margaret Thatcher is breaking the machines
at Dad's work on purpose? I ask my grandad.*

He smiles and says, I shouldn't rule it out, son, I shouldn't.

That was the last year we went to the caravans. We had
days of bright, hard sunshine and the sands to ourselves,
all the way between the castles at Harlech and Criccieth;
that's what it felt like, anyway, especially knowing everyone else was at school or at work or doing their dole. It
was like we'd escaped. School wasn't the same by then.
Jermaine had gone, and I missed Ronnie, and there was
only Paul left to bicker with in between lessons. Rodney
and Michael and their class were off to secondary school.
I was already trying to find excuses not to go to school at
all. Later, when I stopped going altogether, it was easy to
say it was because of what happened to my dad but I'd
already begun to daydream about not going. I imagined
days stretched out in front of me like the wide green valleys
of Wales, free. I talked to Michelle, I suppose. She had her
own problems then. Her dad had come back to live with
them and the house got raided.

She told me about it one wet break-time when we sat and
watched the rain like waves breaking against the window.
I imagined we were on a boat, sailing far away, down the
cut to the river, down the river to the sea.

The policeman, the fat one, sat on his head, she said.

What did you do?

I hid under the table in the kitchen. The police had him in the hall. Michael tried to kick one of em.

Did he?

Yeah, me mom tried to stop him and he kicked a hole in the kitchen door.

Shit.

Michael hates the police.

What happened to yer dad?

They took him off.

What did they want him for?

She took a while to answer, just looked at the rain.

I doh know, really. He was looking after something for somebody, I think.

He still looks after things for people, Isaac. He comes in the pub for his pint of Mickey Mouse every few weeks. He makes the kids laugh, his grandkids, loves them in his way, forgets their birthdays then sticks a roll of twenty pound notes in my hand at odd times. Sometimes Michelle pretends to be out when she sees him limping along from the bus stop. I like him, but then I never had to live with him on and off for twenty years.

That holiday at the caravans, we went on a day trip on the train from Porthmadog and had the whole carriage to ourselves, could see for miles across the lakes and mountains. I remember the Sunday afternoon we left, looking out the back window of the car as we drove across the causeway away from Porthmadog, with the Ffestiniog train puffing steam alongside us and the shadows of clouds making patterns on the hills across the water. I looked back; back at the sun dropping down behind the mountains until we drove into the dark of a plantation of fir trees.

A few weeks later the factory where my dad worked closed down.

It's the night before the royal wedding. Everyone has been given the day off to watch the wedding but at my dad's work they said not to come back at all. They've run out of money and orders for things made of steel so that's that, everyone has to go home and go on the dole. I'm not meant to be listening. I sit upstairs and hear my mum and dad talking. There's nothing much else to do, anyway.

It cor goo on like this. I'll pick summat up. Things ull pick up in the autumn.

My dad is trying to sound cheerful, I can tell. My mum sighs.

Yer say that but where's the pick-up gonna be? Where's it gonna pick up? There ay no sign at all. The onny sign is of things gerrin worse. Me dad says he reckons there's a couple of hundred more going at Cinderheath. They'll shut the whole thing, yer know. Patent Shaft. Round Oak next. Iss gonna get worse. I'm onny repeating what yow've said yerself, Francis. I doh know. I'm tellin yer own words back to yer.

Yome telling me yer dad's words back to me.

Tell me yer doh think they'm true.

We'll be okay.

How will we be okay? How will we?

Doh get upset.

But I am upset.

We'll be okay.

Yer keep sayin that, but how?

I'll get summat. There's always work somewhere.

Try tellin that to the millions out of work.

It ay millions.

It bloody is millions. Even they say that. They fiddle the figures any road. I'm onny repeatin yer own words back to yer. Yer said this to Johnny the other night.

Iss just talk.

What, so yer doh mean what yer say now? Look outside. Yer can see what it's like. Yer know what it's like.

Okay. Calm down.

I want yer to tell me how it's gonna be different for us. This bloody mortgage. I tode yer we should've stayed on the council list.

Doh start that now.

Start what? Start to think about how we'm gonna pay the mortgage on a house we could barely afford in the first place.

All right. I've tode yer it ull be all right.

But how? Yow live in cloud cuckoo land. All that talk of another house and we can barely afford this one. Well, thass over now, thass finished. I doh want to hear any more talk of it.

Look, you said to look out the winder. Think about it. If me an Harry Robertson, or folks like him, goo for the same job, who's gonna get it, eh? If it's me against twenty, thirty folks round here it ull be me that gets the job. We'll be okay. I'll make it okay. I'll get summat else.

My dad says it'll be okay over and over and strokes my mum's hair; I can see the reflection in the hall mirror.

I'll get another job, he says.

He didn't get another job, but even if he had, things might not have worked out. Paul Hill's dad got stopped at GKN, then started on at another place, a galvanizer's down by

Burnt Tree, and he was finished on his first day there. It messed his dole up for ages afterwards and meant Paul and his mum almost got evicted from their flat because Paul's dad paid their rent after the divorce. This happened about the same time Paul split my head open when the Falklands War was on. He told me years later when we bumped into each other at the job centre, where else, that the whole thing with his dad's work was why he had been so angry. I told him not to worry about it, that there was a lot of water under the bridge.

Yer know what's gooin on?

I nod. She knows I've been listening.

Try not to worry, darling, she says. Everything will be okay.

I nod again, knowing full well that she doesn't mean it. She smoothes down my smart clothes on the hanger on the back of my door: Farah trousers and a check shirt. They're for the royal wedding. For a family who doesn't even believe we should have a queen, or a king for that matter, we're doing a good show of it. I've got a new pair of shoes and new haircut. We are going round to my nan and grandad's house to watch the wedding on telly and then to Cinderheath, to the football club, for a Fun Day afterwards. There's going to be a party and barbecue and games. There'll be a bouncy castle and a five-a-side competition at the other end, with things like egg and spoon races between games. This seems a lot of fuss to me, for a boring wedding, for Prince Charles and his big ears. There shouldn't even be a royal family; we should get rid of kings and queens and lords and all that and have a republic.

That's what I thought our family thought. That's what Johnny told me. Instead, we're getting all worked up about a wedding when it seems to me that we've got other things to worry about.

Don't worry about anything. We'll have a nice day to-morrow, eh? My mum flattened down the hair on the top of my head.

You need to put your kit in your sports bag. You can change for the races and things when we're at the ground. You'll enjoy that.

Can I just go in me kit?

No, we've been over this, Sean. Everyone will have their nice clothes on to start with, for the wedding and the party. Then you can change. That's what Uncle Johnny's doing, everyone.

Even Johnny's been sucked in. He said for weeks that he was having nothing to do with it, that he wasn't coming with us, that he'd sit out the back in the quiet and do a bit of painting on his day off. My nan had rolled her eyes and called him a misery and my grandad had shrugged and said, Suit yerself. Then the club phoned him up and asked him to go in goal for one of the teams in the five-a-side competition and suddenly he was all for it.

Why am we having a party if we don't even believe in the royal family? I ask him.

Ah, well, he says. It'll be a nice party and yer mum and nan'll enjoy it. If I play well they might ask me to play again next season.

But I think it's wrong. They spend all their money on this wedding and there's loads of people with no money and who are unemployed and it's their fault, the rich people's fault.

You said because they live like they do that poor people have got no jobs and things. You said no wonder people was rioting. I thought you was gonna do a protest.

Thass true but, Johnny says and then he shrugs. Iss a game of football and a few drinks. We'll all be there together. It'll be good. We'll have a nice time. There's plenty of other stuff to protest about. Doh worry abaht it, Sean.

I've been told not to worry about it by every member of my family. I am eleven years old and can see better than any of them that this doesn't make sense. I thought that maybe I would run off on the morning and go and hide over the allotments or even all the way over to the quarries so no one could find me. That could be my protest. But I realize as my mum is laying my clothes out, snuffling back tears, telling me not to worry like that's going to make everything all right, that there is no way I can upset her any more, so I nod when she says I can't go in my kit.

It's a shame I didn't think about her feelings more later on, that's all I can say now.

It was brilliant, the day of the royal wedding. We all watched the service in the front room at my nan and grandad's. Johnny was right that my mum and nan really loved it, even before we got to the party. They talked about how beautiful Princess Diana looked and cried through the service.

Years later, when my mum was ill, I drove her down to London in the days after Diana died. It was one of the last trips she ever made, in fact. It was a few weeks after I came back, maybe not even that. My mum placed flowers on the Mall. I took some photos. There's one of them up behind the bar now. She looks too thin. You can see the smoke rising from the candles people had lit and the garlands that had been laid to Hindu gods. When I bent down near the spot where my mum laid her flowers there was a card with a picture of Saint Francis on it; the same image that used to hang up above the telly before Margaret Thatcher shamed him down. I felt the tears well up and I turned away from the card and moved towards my mum as if to hold her up. But she was holding me up.

My dad and grandad drink beer at the kitchen table.

Watch what yome having. Yow'll be having plenty of that after, my nan warns my grandad.

He groans and nods at Prince Philip on the screen. Enough to turn yer to drink, he says but he's joking, I think. The people he swears at most when they come on telly are Prince Philip, David Owen, Roy Jenkins, Norman Tebbit, Ron Greenwood, Lester Piggott and Bob Monkhouse. He hates David Owen and Roy Jenkins most of all out of the SDP traitors. If Margaret Thatcher comes on, he walks out of the room. I think it's the biggest insult he can think of, the only thing he can think to do.

Propaganda, he says now, and winks at me.

We never called her Maggie. No one in our family did. It was as if calling her Maggie was something suspect, that it showed you secretly really liked her, thought she was just a pantomime villain that you could shout Out! Out! Out! at and she'd disappear back into the wings. No, better to stick to her full name, or better still, no name at all, a look and we'd know who you meant. She was always there, anyway; you didn't have to name her.

He killed her, yer know. My grandad says this to me late one night when I'm sitting with him in the kitchen getting him warm after bringing him home from the pub. Johnny's upstairs putting my grandad's electric blanket on. For a moment I think he means my dad. Then I think he must be talking about my mum. The anniversary is a few weeks away.

Who?

That bastard, Philip.

What?

He had her bumped off. They think we'm all stupid.

Oh, right.

They should get rid on the lot of em. Them, the royal family, the House of Lords, the Tory Party, the City, all on em. They tek us for fools. They know we'm fools. We must be to put up with it all.

All right, Grandad, doh work yerself up now. Try not to worry about it.

Not worry?

He looks around the room blinking. He takes his glasses off and cleans them on the edge of his jacket and looks at the corner of the room; first with his glasses off, then with his glasses on.

They killed her.

He is talking about my mum. He never does. He'll talk about my nan all the time, never mentions my mum; sometimes he even says things like, when yer dad was alive, but he never mentions my mum.

I'll tell yer another thing, son.

What, Grandad?

Yer should've bloody shot her when yer had the chance.

He has never mentioned it before, never made any reference to what happened, or didn't happen in the end, not a word in twenty years or more. Johnny is coming downstairs. He will put my grandad to bed. Michelle asked me to be quick. Lily wants a bedtime story before I go back behind the bar.

Yer know he voted for em, Grandad? Me dad? When her was first elected, me dad voted Tory.

I don't know why I said this, wanted to tell him, after all these years. Confirm his suspicions, I suppose. He nods.

My old man used to vote for em. He got his vote after the war. The first war this is, 1918. He wouldn't have been allowed afower then. Not all men could vote. Went off to vote Tory wi no shoes on his feet.

Johnny comes down the stairs.

Iss cold in here, Dad, he says as he comes in the room, shivers. We'll get the heating on now the dark nights am here.

Johnny sits on the back step cleaning his boots and putting his keeper's bag ready.

Doh yer wanna come and watch the wedding? my mum says, teasing Johnny. She has got two drinks, a glass of sherry, the same as my nan, and a glass of gin and orange on the kitchen table.

Johnny saved a penalty from Derek Dougan, the old Wolves and Villa player, in the charity shoot-out in the afternoon, and I won the eighty metres sprint. Rodney James tripped at the start and couldn't catch up with me. Derek Dougan gave me a medal. We had a great time. Johnny had too many to drink after playing football all afternoon in the sun. When we got back to the house he walked straight down the entry, out into the back garden and was sick over the back wall into the allotments. He'd let me have a few sips off his pint while he was drinking with some of the Cinderheath players.

They've onny been drinking lager. I doh know whass up with him, my grandad said. Even now, despite being regularly presented with the facts, my grandad believes that lager is not as strong as darker beer, thinks of it more as a soft drink, like Coke, which he also hates.

We'll never hear the last of this bloody penalty, either. My grandad was drunk too. I wouldn't mind but Derek Dougan had had a couple of pints when he took it. I thought it was gonna end up through the clubhouse winders.

It was a great save, Johnny shouted from the garden. What a save! he said.

How about the ones yer let in? Yer day stop that one from Tommy Catesby, he's onny got one leg.

Tom Catesby had played for Wolves but then got injured. My grandad worked with him for a while at Cinderheath. He got him to sign his autograph in Duncan Edwards' book, *Tackle Soccer This Way*. He'd stood and had a drink with him after the five-a-side penalties. My grandad said I could have the book when he died, but that wouldn't be for a good while yet. This was true: it's still there in the bookcase in the hallway, next to the stairlift.

And he was wearing slip-on shoes!

My mum and nan talked about Diana's dress again and my mum said how she looked like a real princess and how the happiest day of her own life had been her wedding day and then she kissed my dad. She was drunk too. My grandad started to sing 'The Red Flag' out of the bathroom window, his voice drifting out across the allotments and houses and dwindling furnaces. He'd locked the door so my nan couldn't get in there to tell him to shut up.

'I'm afraid some things will get worse before they get better. But after almost any major operation you feel worse before you convalesce. But you don't refuse the operation when you know that without it you won't survive. Is this perhaps beginning to get through?'

I wonder if it was a relief at first, for my dad, after the months of arriving home and then having to turn around and go back to work, months of the phone ringing in the middle of the night. At first, it must have felt something like a holiday. He got his colour back, was less grey, sat in the sun with his shirt off, came and met me on the way home from school in the afternoons.

One day, right near the end of term, I was sitting outside the Spar at the top of Crow Street with Michelle. We were sharing an ice lolly that we'd scraped some change together for, one of those fancy ones that came out around then, a pina colada. We were sitting on the milk crates out the front of the shop, in the shade under the awning to stop the lolly melting.

My dad walked from across the road. He was wearing a white shirt with the sleeves rolled back, holding a golf club he must've found in the shed at my nan and grandad's, letting the club head touch the ground softly as he walked. It glinted in the sun, making him look like a gent with a silver cane.

He smiled when he saw us, pointed the golf club at me as he crossed the road.

Thass my dad, I said to Michelle.

I thought we was gooin to the park? he says, pointing the golf club towards me and blinking as he reaches the shade. He's still smiling, though. It's not like we've made it a rule, it's just that on the days since we've come back to school after the royal wedding, since he lost his job, he's met me on the way home and we've walked over to the park.

Okay.

Doh get up, there's no rush, enjoy yer lolly, he says, and then he says, Hello, darling, to Michelle.

She says hello and he stands on the shop step for a moment, looking at us.

What yer got? He nods at the lollipop.

A pina colada, we say together. He laughs.

Thass a good un, he says. When he comes back out of the shop he's holding a carrier bag in one hand and a lolly in the other. He hands the new one to Michelle.

Here yam, chick. Doh let Sean ate all yer lolly.

I can feel Michelle looking down the hill after us and smiling as we walk towards the park.

We take turns at hitting the old seven iron from the shed, that my dad has spent the afternoon polishing, until I can get the ball to go in the air and in the same long arc as my dad. I copy the way he links his little fingers on the club shaft.

Head down, he says. Look at the ball.

He says, Look at the ball, whenever we play anything. We go back and forth at the far end of the park. I see the ball hanging in the air in front of the castle and then drop against the green pattern of trees.

Thass it, perfect, my dad says. He says we'll go over the pitch and putt with Johnny one day, maybe even persuade my grandad.

*Iss a useful skill, he says, hitting a decent seven iron.
Good for business meetings and the like, he says, smiling
to himself.*

That couple of months he was first off, he'd meet me, or
take me over the park, with a ball or a bat, all different
sports. So we'd knock the football back and forth across
the long grass, or nip through the hole in the fence to the
tennis courts. One night he bought a Frisbee along, the
next a proper hard, red cricket ball with a raised seam,
showed me how to hold it right, with my middle finger
on the seam, so I could get it to move when it landed,
try to nip it away, he said, side-on more, Sean, use your
shoulder, get yer arm high, get side-on as you bowl, thass
it, great stuff.

We went straight to my nan and grandad's that night
and I remember my dad tossing the ball into my grandad's
lap when we got there and my grandad telling me that the
first time he met my dad wasn't when my mum brought
him home for a Sunday tea of tinned salmon and peaches,
which was a story I'd heard a few times, but earlier on that
afternoon when he'd been sat in a deckchair with a pint
of mild by the Dudley pavilion, watching this young kid
come in and bowl fast, thinking he's a good un, this un;
then seeing him come through the front door that night,
with his hair combed, standing shyly next to my mum with
everyone staring at him. My dad stopped playing cricket
because of work, to start saving for a house.

He was a good bowler, yer dad, quick.

He'd learned to bowl in Quarry End at the field at the
bottom of the farm, before it was swallowed by the quarry.
They used to play with stones and bat with branches from

the trees, that was what my dad told me, but he was laughing when he said it.

There's a cricket club every morning for a couple of weeks on the school playground. I tear in and bowl fast and the kids shout, Goo on, Sean, as I start my run-up. I'm faster even than Rodney James and can bowl out Michael Campbell and Mani Singh. This is all thanks to my dad showing me how. We keep the club going all summer on our own, a milk crate at one end of the pitch, a set of stumps painted on the wall at the other end. Mani comes in with a pot of white paint one morning and we go over the stumps and paint lines for the creases on the playground concrete.

One afternoon I get home and the garage door is open and I walk through and my dad has set up a barbecue outside. Barbecues are all the rage since the royal wedding. The garden smells of smoke and sausages. My mum sits in the swing, laughing, wearing big sunglasses and a skirt; she has her legs out in the sun. She holds a frothy yellow drink in a pint glass. On the table next to the barbecue my dad has slices of pineapple lined up and a bottle of white rum. He passes me a slice of pineapple; the juice runs down my arms as I eat it, like the way a lolly melts and drips.

Pina colada, my dad says, laughing, and my mum raises her glass.

I think of them together now, trapped in that oblong of sunshine out the back of the house on Elm Drive. I started to like the house more, with us all there together, without the threat of us moving away somewhere soon. There was no talk of that. My dad had to get a job first. When

September came things were bound to pick up, that's what people said then.

Not long after that my grandad lost his job. He turned up one morning and instead of a sandwich and cup of tea at breakfast, all the workers got called to a meeting and that was it. He was told to get his stuff and go home.

They'm putting the fire out, he said to me later, trying to explain what was going on.

I knew full well what was going on by then. Cinderheath was closing. All the men had to go home. There were no jobs any more. That was it.

I am sitting watching Barbara Castle flit around her cage while reading my Roy of the Rovers Summer Special *when my grandad appears at the back door, not at three o'clock in the afternoon, but at half past ten in the morning.*

My grandad says, Where's yer nan, Sean? as he walks through the kitchen.

Upstairs, putting new sheets on the bed, I say, I'd helped her get them in from the line, and I can see something is badly wrong because he keeps walking straight through in his boots that he always leaves by the back door before having a wash in the sink when he comes home from work.

After he's told my nan what's happened, he has to tell Harry, who rattles the back door because he's seen my grandad come home early. Then my mum comes back from cleaning, so he tells her too. My grandad gives my mum a hug and says it doesn't matter, he'll be retired now, he's fifty-nine and who'd give him a job? They'd have more sense than that.

I've got more time to work on the garden and the allotment, he says. After he's had two cups of tea and a glass of whisky he says that he worked there for forty-two years and they'd said get yer stuff, that's it, don't come back ever again. There's been rumours, he says, rumours, gossip, that's all he thought it was, even though it's been happening everywhere else. Later, still sitting at the kitchen table, he raises his glass of whisky to Johnny, who comes in from work with the paper where there is a picture of the Cinderheath gantry on the front page and THE END *written in big letters. My grandad does a toast to being retired.*

Yow can keep me in the manner to which I've become accustomed, he says to Johnny.

I think you've had enough now, Dad, eh? my mum says, when he pours another glass and starts dozing off in his chair and he nods, which he never does normally. On a Sunday he usually says I've onny had a drop, when you can see he's drunk from the way he's standing all leaned over to one side. Then he goes to make a cup of tea and then my nan takes over and he goes off to bed.

Nice new sheets, my nan says to him, stirring the milk in his tea.

The next day he smashed the carriage clock that he'd been given for twenty-five years' service on the back step. It used to stand on the mantelpiece in the front room. Not even my dad was able to put it back together again when my nan showed it to him that afternoon. My grandad went down to the allotment. My dad took out two little springs and put them in his pocket.

Put it in the bin, he said.

'It is time to change people's approach to what governments should do for them, and what they do for themselves. It is time to persuade ourselves that only by our own efforts can we halt our national decline.'

My dad has a clever idea for getting work. It's Charlie Clancey's idea, really. He gets a message to my dad through my grandad, stops by at the house on his round. With all the works closed down there are big machines left in all the empty factories. Some of the machines are being taken apart and used for scrap, which is where Charlie comes in, or they're being shipped off to other countries that might use them in the future. There's other stuff as well, like copper pipes and steel cable, but my dad's new job, if he wants it, is to take the big machines apart, the ones that aren't moving all in one piece. Charlie wants my grandad to work with him too.

Yow woh get another job at yower age, Jack, not with the way things am.

All right, steady on, I ay that ode, Charlie, but I'll tell yer summat, I'm too ode for that sort of carry-on. I am retired, thanks very much. I would pass on yer offer to Francis but I'd tell him to tell yer where to goo, I'm telling yer that now. If yow want to speak to him yerself, well, thass between yow an him.

When Charlie leaves they shake hands as normal, but my grandad looks at the space where Charlie had sat and where he left through the back door for a long time; he sits there staring.

Charlie says, Think abaht it, Jack, through the kitchen window as he walks down the path. My grandad keeps staring.

He's not really retired. He can't get his pension until he's sixty-five but retired is what he calls himself. I think he does it so he doesn't have to say he's unemployed. I can tell that my grandad is upset about it all, he reads the paper from cover to cover, and swears at the television. He even agrees with Johnny more.

Thass great news, about Charlie wanting my dad to do some work for him, I say.

My grandad doesn't say anything.

Out the back of my nan and grandad's house things began to change. You didn't see smoke coming out of the works' chimneys any more. The chimneys sat there getting rained on, and over time they took some of them down. The same with the gantry at Cinderheath; it stayed there with crows sitting on it and everything getting rusted in the rain. Things started slipping into the old workings. They put scaffolding up at the top end of Crow Street to hold the houses up. No one was allowed onto the allotments.

My nan and grandad's next door neighbours, the Blowers, died within a few days of each other while all this was going on. I remember because Geraldine came banging on the back door on the morning of her mother's funeral to say she didn't think her dad was breathing. My dad went round there to check and my mum followed with Geraldine, holding her hand.

Thass the way to go, though, I spose, my grandad said later and my nan nodded.

They had a joint funeral in the end, with a horse and carriage that pulled its way up the hill with two coffins. All the curtains on the street were pulled tight across and even the people not going to the funeral stood on their front steps with their heads bowed.

No one could find Albert the tortoise. I wanted him, was sure I'd be allowed to look after him if we could find him, but he was gone, vanished. We thought he'd crept into the abandoned allotments. I stood at the fence one afternoon, daring myself to sneak through and search for him, imagining he'd found lettuce growing wild on one of the overgrown plots or that he'd crawled his way down into the caves somehow. There was no sign and my nerve went. My mum had told me over and over since they put the fences up that if I went in there the earth would swallow me up. The Robertsons' cat, Cleopatra, went the same way, slinked through the fence to look for mice and never came back; perhaps she thought it wasn't worth it, not without Ronnie to look after her.

I thought maybe we could have the Blowers' house, now it was empty, but there was no talk of that. A young couple were moved in, called Trevor and Julie. I thought he was all right; he used to put his thumb up to me when he was out in the garden and say, All right, our kid, but he knocked her around. The police had to come a couple of times. My grandad went round there once when we could hear her screaming. My nan got upset and said that it used to be a nice road and that our row used to be the best of them all. Trevor and Julie got moved out. A bloke called Martin, who worked for my uncle Eric, lived there with his wife Kerry, then bought the house off the council when they got the chance, put a new porch on the front, had the

windows replaced. Their daughter lived there afterwards.
They rent it out now. My grandad says there are all sorts
of comings and goings in the middle of the night. Johnny
tells him not to worry about it, not to get involved.

My mum doesn't want my dad working with Charlie.
  Yow'll get arrested, she says.
  I woh get arrested. Wim being careful.
  *By working for Charlie! Everybody in Dudley knows
what a rogue he is; yow've onny got to mention his name.
I'm surprised yow ay bin stopped already.*
  It ull be okay.
  Yer keep saying that.
  Well, it will. Wim being careful.
  *And it's dangerous, places yer doh know, without the
proper equipment.*
  *What would you rather I do? Tell him to keep his money?
He's helpin us out.*
  *Helpin hisself. It ay even that much, Francis, not really.
I bet Charlie's mekkin a fortune somehow.*
  Arr, cos he looks like a man with a fortune stashed away.
  *I know that my dad is being sarcastic because of the
way that Charlie always has the same clothes on, that hat
with the feather in it and a check jacket, with his trousers
held up with string, or a leather belt tied in a knot, not
fastened with a buckle, and the way he smells, like the day
I saw him at the tip, of all the rubbish and rag and bone.
He lives in a broken-down shed on his scrapyard down
by the canal. His horses live out behind it.*
  *Doh believe what he looks like. Me mother says he's
worth a fortune.*
  What?

He's got it buried under the house. That's what my mother told me.

They are laughing now. I can hear them. That's better.

I cor believe it's come to this, my mum is saying.

Yow've done a good shift today, son, yome a good worker. My dad is doing an impersonation of Charlie now. My mum and dad have both had a bit to drink. Yow tek care o that lovely wench o yowers.

Now he's gone back to his own voice. A good day's work, I ask yer! Charlie Clancey! Yome right about what it's come to.

I'm glad they're happy now. Every morning my dad goes out to work as normal. I know that he leaves the car somewhere different every day, so that it can't be traced by government agents, like the SAS. He walks to get picked up somewhere by Charlie in the van. Each night Charlie phones to say where the next day's pick-up point is, like the end of Cromwell Green Road, or the entrance to Buffery Park, or at the front of the Lion, and my dad works out where to leave the car or whether to walk to the pick-up. I'm worried that the phone is tapped, though. That's when the government records any conversations you have on the telephone and comes to arrest you. Johnny told me all about it. In the book he's reading a man got arrested by the police and then put on trial, but he didn't know what crime he'd been charged with, so he had to stand up in the court to defend himself not knowing what he'd done wrong.

Some days my dad has to drive to wherever they're working and then hide the car there. On those days he has to pick up the other workers too because Charlie likes to use the horse and cart. Charlie gives him a bit extra for that. If the work for Charlie stopped we'd have to sell the car anyway; the house would be next. I'm not meant to know that.

On the days when my dad drives, my mum stands behind the front door or walks into the dining room and pulls back the net curtain to look out at the street. Sometimes she stands there for ages, just looking; then sometimes she goes and pours a glass of gin.

So if anyone asks yer at school, Sean?

I say he ay got a job.

He hasn't, say he hasn't, not he ay.

All right, he hasn't got a job.

Exactly. Because he hasn't, but he'll get one again soon. He's just doing a few favours for Charlie while he's not at work.

The work for Charlie is such a big secret because it's against the law, to work and get dole, except the law's stupid and anyway the laws are being made by Margaret Thatcher, so it's probably better to break them. It's against the law to take the machines if they don't belong to you, as well. There are people in our road that my mum is worried might phone the government if they think my dad is working and claiming dole. If anyone does that and we know who it is I'm going to make a petrol bomb and sneak out and set fire to their house.

'I am very anxious about
the West Midlands because
I recognize that the people
there think they have
suffered.'

Months went by and this was how we lived. Some weeks there was no work from Charlie at all, but usually there was some. In the slow weeks, my dad sometimes worked on the cars for Harry Robertson.

Harry would swap bits from different cars around all the time. He would then stand there looking at the parts he'd laid out on the pavement or inside a car's bonnet, scratching his head. Sometimes he'd sell one of the cars and stand shaking hands with the new owner in the street, trying not to look too relieved.

Nothing but old bangers, my nan, who knew nothing about cars, would say. Meks the whole street look a mess.

Sometimes my dad would help Harry fix one of his puzzles. My dad could fix anything. He stood there looking at the broken engine for a long time and then he'd move a few things around, or get Harry to fetch something from one of the other cars or his toolbox, and the car would start up again. If Harry sold a car that my dad had helped him on then Harry would give my dad some money. He'd take the notes out of his cigarette packet while they stood in the entry and pass them to my dad. It was the same as with Charlie; they had to check for government agents. I always kept a look out. My dad told me not to worry. I pictured the SAS coming from out of the allotments or over the rooftops and wondered how I wasn't meant to worry about that.

When the dark nights and bad weather came there was less work of any sort. My mum and dad talked in whispers in the kitchen and sometimes I listened, sometimes not. They talked about money. My dad talked about moving, moving away to find work. I tried to imagine it. If we had to go I hoped it would be Australia or somewhere. My mum didn't want to move.

I will move, she said, but not far, not far, Francis, our lives am here.

There's nothing here.

Our lives am here, Francis. Our lives.

It's February. I watch the clouds coming. They don't come like usual; they come from the wrong direction. I tell my mum. Usually, if you're out the front at my nan and grandad's you can see the wind blowing the clouds past Dudley, they come, high and white, past the castle and Top Church. The best place to see them is from the top of Cawney Bank; you can see them drifting on their way. They're called the Severn Jacks. Cromwell's soldiers must have watched them, sitting here on the same hill, firing their cannons at the castle. Shakespeare used to watch them from the river bank in Stratford. The weather always comes that way. It starts somewhere near America, near Jamaica, and comes across the Atlantic and picks up rain on the way. It rains on Ireland and Wales and the clouds come up the Severn and sometimes they rain on us. Not today, though. The clouds come the other way. My mum's not interested what direction the clouds are coming from. She says it looks like snow, though.

The clouds are a strange shape, dark on the undersides and there's a glow around them on the horizon. When I go out it feels strange and still. I think maybe something has happened, like a nuclear disaster or something. The cloud isn't in a mushroom but it billows like in the films of nuclear bombs on telly. If the weather comes the other way it's from the mountains in Russia, the Union of the Soviet Socialist Republics. There's nothing between us and those mountains, freezing cold air coming across Polish and German plains for hundreds of miles and all the flat land east of us, like Grantham, where Margaret Thatcher grew up. It must've been cold growing up on a flat plain like that with no hills for shelter. I think for a moment that it's the end of the world, that we'll see planes or angels come flying out of the dark clouds. Everyone thinks there might be a war at some point, but people don't talk about it that much.

Wim done for with that clown with his finger on the button, my grandad says about Ronald Reagan, especially with her egging him on. He means Margaret Thatcher. There's a button you can press, if you are President of the United States or General Secretary of the Communist Party of the Union of Soviet Socialist Republics, and fire off all the nuclear missiles you want at different cities. It's called Global Thermo-Nuclear War.

Sometimes I look on the map and pick out all the places that will get bombed that I'll probably never visit, like Chicago and Vladivostok and Aberdeen. I've invented a game where I roll two dice to get a number, say eleven, and pretend that's the number of nuclear bombs each side has got and then I work out where they'll drop them. I look at the atlas and work out the best places. The first few are easy, like Moscow and Leningrad and New York, Washington and London, but then it gets harder. The places that will get bombed are capital cities, and places with army bases, or ports, and then cities with lots of factories. If Margaret Thatcher works fast enough all our factories will close and we'll be safe because we won't be rich or powerful enough to deserve a nuclear bomb. It's something to think about.

And, actually, both sides have got enough bombs to blow the whole world up so it doesn't really matter what order they do it in. Plus, even if the bombs don't drop right on us we'll have to live through a nuclear winter and get radiation sickness or live in the caves underground for hundreds of years, like my grandad says we will.

It's only a game for me, though. I got the idea from another game in Johnny's room called Risk. In that game you have to try and take over the whole world, like England did when it ruled India and Africa and Australia.

I'm gooin back out, my dad says.

What now?

I said I'd see Charlie. There's summat he wants me to look at.

Now?

Now.

Yer tea's ready. Iss nearly dark.

He wants it dark.

Am yer gooin out in that thin coat? Get yer big coat from the garage.

My dad winks at me and my mum goes looking out the back for the coat he does the garden and washes the car in. I want to ask if I can go with him. I know he'll say no and so I don't say anything.

The east wind doesn't bring bombs or angels either; it brings snow, and it starts snowing while my dad stands there with the door open, waiting for my mum to find his coat, with the light beginning to go.

The snowflakes are so big that they make a noise when they land on my coat. I stand with my hands out, my mouth open, catching snowflakes. In no time the drive is covered, the cars; it's dark as my dad walks off down the road. My mum calls me in and I sit with a hot water bottle and look out of the front window at the snow falling in the glow of the streetlight. Down on the main road I see cars skidding past at first, then the flashing orange lights of the grit van, then no cars at all. I know there'll be no school tomorrow and I hug the hot water bottle, pleased. But all the time I'm thinking of how I watched my dad walk down the road into the snow and how I could see the shape of his body grow fainter and fainter, the snow falling in his footsteps, until he disappeared.

It's how I think of him now, I suppose. I picture him with the snow slowly erasing him; like a wave looming above him, white horses spitting and menacing to bring our whole life crashing down. I pick these things out now, that in another, different life wouldn't have registered at all.

'But let me be brutally frank. Things which are welcome to one community are unwelcome to another.'

Charlie Clancey is down the police station. He was arrested in the snow. My nan phones my mum to tell her. The machines they've been dismantling, the iron they save from the dead factories, it's not theirs to take. No one else wants it, though. Margaret Thatcher's decided nothing is any use in them, so it's rag and bone really; Dad and Charlie are like the Jawas cleaning up old droids in Star Wars. That's how I see it, anyway. They're doing a good job. The police don't see it the same.

They come for my dad on the day I go back to school after the snow. The snow is hard and packed at the sides of the road, dazzling in the February sun. I know it will turn to mud and slush. There's no morning raid or SAS coming through the windows. They knock on the door and my dad goes off to the police station in Dudley to be questioned. They don't arrest him. One of the policemen said that they want to arrest him, that they've been watching him, that they'll get him eventually, like they'll get them all. The policeman said that quietly, by the desk in the station, under the picture of the queen, not when they were doing the questioning. I hear my dad telling my mum this, sitting at my listening post on the stairs.

Fat bastard, my dad says, about the policeman.

*I bet he's the same one that sat on Michelle's dad's head.
I'm going to tell her.*

Charlie's still in there, poor bloke.

*Fuck Charlie, my mum says. I've never heard my mum
swear before, ever. I doh wanna hear his fuckin name in
this house. Iss stealing, Francis, theft; iss wrong.*

*This house is why I was doing it. Any road, how's it
stealing if they'm gonna leave them machines there to rust?*

*I doh care about the house. I doh care. I was happy in
the flat. I'd be happy anywhere. I've tode yer. I doh want
a big house. I never wanted to buy this one. All this wanting more. All this talk of more. Houses and cars. We cor
afford it, any road. Even in work. I wouldn't want it if
we could. I was happy, Francis. I was happy.*

*She's shouting and then she does a big sob and I know
she's crying. I can't tell what my dad's doing. He's not
banging the kitchen table or anything like that.*

Charlie was doing us a favour, he says.

My mum laughs now but she's not really laughing.

*Yow could still go to prison, yer know that, doh yer? Just
because they ay charged yer today. This ull go on and on.
Yow heard what that policeman said to yer.*

Charlie woh say nuthin.

Charlie this, Charlie that.

*She grunts now and I hear a slap and she's trying to hit
my dad. I can hear them shuffling across the kitchen; the
stool scrapes across the floor then topples over. My dad's
going Sh, sh, sh to her. She takes a big breath.*

*Yow used to laugh at him. Charlie the tatter. Charlie
the gypo. Now Charlie's the onny thing between us and
losing the house, the only thing between you and going to
prison. If you think I'm the sort of person who wants yer*

to risk going to prison so we can live in this stupid house you don't know me at all. Yer doh know me.

I want us to get on, you know. I want a nice house. Yow want one too. Woss wrong with that, wi wanting things?

What is the matter with yer? I ay changed, Francis. Iss yow thass changed. I knew it. Yow asked for this. I hope yome happy with it now, I really do. I doh care what house we live in.

I hear my dad pick up the stool and put it back in its place.

I was doing it for you, he says, for us.

Yer was doin it for yerself, my mum says, and then the back door slams shut.

They stopped speaking. They'd talk to each other in front of me but they'd avoid each other, even in the house. My dad slept on the settee downstairs then would go up to bed when my mum got up to get me started for school. He'd stay in bed until late in the day until my mum went up to see my nan or to do her cleaning. I know she'd take him a cup of tea up sometimes, try to get him going.

I went to school in the slush and watched for the police from the front window when I got home.

'We are also doing a good
deal to cushion the effect of
change in the old industries.'

Now there's a war, a real war. Not like the one with the IRA or Iranian gunmen or against the rioters. We're going to fight a war against Argentina. Argentina invaded the Falkland Islands, which belong to us, even though they're almost on the other side of the world, right down in the South Atlantic, near to Cape Horn, the tip of South America, on the way to Antarctica. They're rocky islands in the middle of a rough, freezing sea, with more penguins and sheep than people, but the people speak English and they think they're English and have red telephone boxes and stuff like that, even though the nearest proper country is Argentina. This all comes from the days of Empire, when English soldiers went off and captured places and England ruled over them all, ruled the waves, like in the song. That was how we got so rich.

They'm bloody welcome to em. What use am they to we here? Nobody knowed where they was till yesterday.

My grandad says this to Johnny. They're not arguing. Johnny is nodding his head.

I thought they was in Scotland, my nan says.

The reporter on the telly is saying that the generals in Argentina might have made a miscalculation about Margaret Thatcher's appetite for a fight.

You've only got to look in her eyes, shining like Michael Campbell's and Mani Singh's that night when they had that massive fight by the Spar, when the police came, the same ones that took me and Ronnie home, and we all had to run off, to see that she wants a fight. One look at the television for the last three years with Margaret Thatcher talking about strikes and people rioting and the IRA and anyone, really, who didn't think like her, should have shown the Argentinians how much she'll enjoy a war.

The SAS'll go, I say.

I hope they sink, Johnny says.

Watch what yome saying, my nan says. Doh get yerself into any bother.

I doh care, Johnny says.

It was worse for the Argentinians than for us, though. Johnny told me that if you were his age in Argentina you'd be forced to go into the army to go and fight in the Falklands and if you didn't want to go that was no use because you got put into a plane and the plane flew high over Buenos Aires and then dropped you, without a parachute, into the River Plate, These people were called the Disappeared, although everyone knew where they'd gone. Johnny still wanted Argentina to win, though. Our enemy's enemy was our friend, he said.

In the end, though, it was me who was injured in the Falklands War.

Propaganda, thass all it is. They must think we was all born yesterday, my grandad says. Iss all about oil, gas, any road. They think we'm stupid. They'm spending all our oil money on the dole so they need to find some more. Thass all iss about, yow watch what happens.

Just watch what yome saying, my nan says.

I doh care, my grandad says.

We play Falklands War at school. Everyone wants to play as the SAS. I say that I'll play as Argentina. The hut where they put the bins is the Falkland Islands, the slope below the bins is the Atlantic Ocean. I find a carrier bag swirling in the wind and put it on a stick and say it's the Argentinian flag. I prop it on top of the bins and everyone else runs around, trying to get the flag and invade the islands. I'm taller than most of them and the bins are on a slope. I'm looking down on everyone; it's easy to defend these islands. If this is what the real war is like, Argentina will win, I think.

But really I don't want to play the game. We're too old for this sort of silliness. We go to secondary school in September. They're changing the system soon so kids go a year earlier, at eleven, so in a way we should already be there. We're going backwards, acting like little kids playing soldiers. I want to play football like normal.

I've been practising with my left foot against the back wall at home and on Sunday mornings at the edge of the pitches down by the canal with my dad.

The other Sunday, after I told my dad what I was practising, he got me to leave my slipper on my right foot and put my boot on my left, which meant I had to kick the ball with my left foot when he knocked it to me. My slipper got covered in mud and my mum was angry with my dad when we got back. I was worried, especially when she really started shouting, expecting him to lose his temper. It was good he'd come out with me, I thought, but he sat at the kitchen table with his head down so I went up to my mum and said, It ay Dad's fault. Iss how yer train to get good with yer left foot.

She said slippers cost money and that we hadn't got any. That was when I finally realized that we were poor and that Johnny had been right all along. Then she got distracted because I'd said It ay instead of It isn't, and she started telling me that I had to try and speak proper English but in a gentler, calmer voice now. Then she said it wasn't the end of the world and that she could get the slipper clean and she put it in the washing up bowl with some soap powder and poured the kettle over it and it was true, it did get clean. When I turned round to look at my dad sitting at the kitchen table I swear there were tears rolling down his face.

Paul is getting angry. He started off laughing, shouting, Kill the Argies! Kill the Argies! but now he's gone red in the face and is trying to reach up to where the flag is and every time he gets near I push him down the slope. He's the leader of the British Forces, the South Atlantic Task Force. He has pictures of warships and the SAS that he's cut out of the newspaper and brought in to show us all. He's got a cousin in the army who he says might get sent to fight. He's in Ireland now. Paul thinks I'll let him win. Maybe he thinks he's stronger and will win anyway. He's not, though, and he won't.

Hold his arms! Hold his arms! he shouts to the others who still think we're playing, but they can't grab me as I dodge round them.

Paul punches me, hard. I swing a punch back but I miss. He grabs my hair and tries to whack my head against the brick bin shed that is the Falkland Islands. I can't grab

187

his hair. He's had it all shaved off like the soldiers and the skinheads. I bring my head up fast and it smashes him in the face and he goes falling backwards and the others all shout Scrap! Scrap! Scrap! and Ooh! Ooh! Ooh! like we always do when there's a fight. Paul grabs a pole. I think how we're not meant to play around here because of the stuff that the workmen left when they did up the nursery: slabs and bags of concrete and thick metal poles like the one Paul has picked up now. He runs at me with it held over his head and I stop still, freeze. I could dodge, or swing a punch, or try to run away; no one would blame me, it's against the rules to try something like this. But I'm thinking, Come on then, let's fight about your stupid fucking islands and your cousin in the army helping Margaret Thatcher and then Paul smashes the pole over my head.

I know there's blood because there's some on my hands and spots of it on the gravel in front of me. I can't see properly. There's blood in front of my eye and I can't get up off the floor. Everyone screams and runs around. There's a whistle blowing and I can see Pete, the caretaker, wrestling with Paul to get him to drop the iron pole, which goes with a crash onto the floor, like it did on my head.

He's killed him, I hear someone shout, but it's not like when I fell out of the window. I know I'm not dead this time. It's just blood and a clanging in my ears from the iron bar crashing and it sounds like the metal I used to be able to hear being bashed at the works from across the allotments, and then everything goes black.

I come round in Mr Taylor's car. I'm wrapped in a blanket on the back seat and Mrs Jukes, the school secretary, is sitting next to me. She's got a son in the navy on the way to the Falkland Islands. There's a picture of him above her desk in the office with a poppy pinned on it, even though it isn't November, and a Union Jack. For a moment I think that she knows the truth and they're going to drive me off and drop me into the canal from the bridge and I'll be like one of the Disappeared. I'm sick onto the blanket and Mrs Jukes says, It's okay, darling, it's okay, and wipes my mouth with some tissues.

We're at the hospital and a doctor sews my eyelid back on, which was the problem, it was hanging off, and why even Michelle was crying and trying to get at Paul to punch him even when he still had the iron pole in his hands and even though she'd been one of the people shouting Ooh! Ooh! Ooh! and clapping and stamping when we started fighting. She loves a good fight.

I have concussion, a big lump on my head and stitches in my right eyelid and eyebrow.

Paul is in big trouble. I'm allowed back in class, even though I haven't had my stitches out yet but I have to stay in at playtime and go home at dinner. I want to stay off and pretend to have a worse headache than I have, but my mum makes me go. Paul hasn't been allowed back to school yet.

There has to be a meeting at the school now that my concussion's gone. Paul's mum and dad are here, and so are mine. His mum and dad don't live together and his dad lives somewhere on Sledmere with Paul's half-brother and sister. I haven't seen him for ages. He has tattoos all up his arms.

My mum says the most in the meeting. The two dads are silent. Paul's dad and mine nod to each other at the start and now they sit looking at the floor while the women speak to Mr Taylor and Mrs Jones, our teacher. We copy our dads. On the way into the meeting Paul asks me if I'm all right and I nod. The police have been round to Paul's house. They weren't friendly with him this time. He could have been arrested for what happened. My mum wants to know why he hasn't been, why he's being let back into the school, why the victim and the attacker are being treated the same.

He could have been killed, she says over and over.

I know you're upset, Mrs Bull, Mr Taylor says.

Upset? Upset? I'm livid, she says, You send yer child to school thinking they'll be safe. The onny reason yome dealing with it like this is because they was playing where they shouldn't and you wasn't watching em properly. It's all about yerselves and how yer look. I've a good mind to ring the paper up and see what they've got to say about it.

Okay. Mrs Bull, that's enough.

I know he's done wrong but he was provoked, Paul's mum says now. She's looking from me to my mum like she wants to strangle us.

Provoked! What can he have done to provoke an iron bar round the head, like that?

He had a black eye, our Paul. He ay never one to start a fight.

He did have a black eye where I hit him with my head. It's fading now. There's still a little bump on the back of my head where I did it. That bump is nothing to the bump on my forehead. The bit about him never starting a fight is a lie: he likes fighting.

Me and Paul get told to sit outside while they carry on talking. We can hear my mum still saying that I could have been killed. I want her to be quiet now. She's made her point. He was actually trying to kill me, so there's no point saying it. It's what happens in a war.

All right? Paul says again and I nod again.

We shake hands and watch the fish in the tank by the reception window. Our class comes out of assembly and Michelle sees us and comes to walk over and ask us what's going on but Mrs Jukes spots her and says, Where do you think you're going, young lady? and Michelle goes back to the class line glaring at Mrs Jukes.

This was just before they sank the *Belgrano*.

Her's onny havin this war to get bloody re-elected. People gerrin killed all for her vanity.

My grandad shouted at the television. My nan ignored him. She'd told him not to talk about the war in front of me.

A couple of days later *HMS Sheffield* was blown up; there was a picture of it burning on the front of the papers and on the news constantly. It was the ship Mrs Jukes' son was serving on. He died. She was off school the rest of the year, until we left, so we didn't see her again. We had a big assembly with a minute's silence and a school collection for Mrs Jukes. We got told that he died serving his country. I imagined him burning, burning; then drowning in the freezing Atlantic.

I saw her at Merry Hill a few years ago, shuffling along with her daughter. There were soldiers there in their desert uniforms, collecting. You see them around much more now. I looked to see if she put anything in their collecting tins but she stared through the open doors of Marks and Spencer's. I thought of her picturing her son burning, drowning, full fathom five, every morning, every day, all the time, over and over in her head. That's what it would be like. That's what it was like now, I supposed, as she walked through the shopping centre, holding her daughter's arm.

One of the soldiers put a sticker on Josh. We nodded and said thanks and then sneaked it off him back at the car when he wasn't looking.

My grandad watched the ship burning and muttered that at least the men he'd fought with had been dying for a reason. That was only the second time I'd ever heard him mention the war. There was a shoebox of medals upstairs in the back of my nan and grandad's bedroom. He'd fought in Sicily and Italy. The only other time I'd heard him talk about it was with my uncle Freddie when he came to visit from Australia. Uncle Freddie had fought, too. He'd been shot in the leg in the Normandy landings. By an American, he used to say.

'Without order fear becomes master and the strong and the violent become a power in the land.'

I know where there's a gun. I'm not meant to know but I do. This gun's from the war. It's in that metal box on a shelf in the shed. I've seen it once before. We'd all been somewhere, for a big meal, celebrating my uncle Freddie's visit from Australia. Everyone had come back to my nan and grandad's. It was August. I had my wooden boomerang with pictures of koala bears to play with. Everyone had drinks in the house and out in the garden. Late in the afternoon my grandad walked down into the allotments with my uncle Freddie and said he'd show him something. He must have been a bit drunk. You could hear everyone laughing back at the house and we walked through the wild spiky grass and foxgloves through the allotments. I was still little, couldn't quite see over the grass at that time of year.

When we got to the hut on the allotment, Grandad pulled a bottle of whisky from underneath the workbench and poured two glasses for him and Freddie. Freddie was laughing, always laughing. Then my grandad reached up to the high shelf, the one right under the ceiling where the old tins of paint and creosote were, and reached to the back. He pulled out a blue tin box, with a key in the lid.

Do you remember what this is? my grandad asked my uncle Freddie with a grin, like he'd forgotten I was there, which he had, I think.

He turned the key and opened the box, took out a cloth bag with all rags and torn up bits of newspaper in it, and it smelled of grease, and then he pulled the gun out of the bag. He pointed it off into the distance over the factory wall. Somewhere off towards West Bromwich.

Jesus, what yer kept that fower? my uncle Freddie asked.

My grandad shrugged. Never know when yer might need it, eh?

Yer should get rid on it. See Charlie with it. He'll get rid on it for yer. It ay safe keeping it in here. An the bullets with it still, look yer. It ay safe. Yome meant to have a licence, ay yer?

My grandad laughed at this. I day think yow'd be so up on English law, Fred. Not after all this time.

My grandad pointed the gun towards Tipton. Then he took the whisky, poured two more drinks to finish the bottle and wandered over to the fence and stood the bottle on the fencepost, paced backwards with the gun like he'd seen in cowboy films.

Come on, Jack. Iss the middle of the afternoon. Yow cor fire a gun aht here. Yow'll have the police here. What about Sean?

My grandad stretched his arm out in front of him, aiming at the bottle.

It still fires, yer know.

Jesus, Jack, doh be so saft.

The bottle wasn't balanced properly on the fencepost and it wobbled slightly. It was White Horse whisky. I stood in the hut doorway, to the side and out of the way. Everything was still and very hot. The backs of the houses seemed a long way away over the tall grass. The sun shone on the windows.

He still had the gun in his hand and was holding it out towards the chimneys.

I oil it sometimes. I tode yer I've tried it a couple of times. Tek it apart like they used to show we. I doh know why. Still.

He lowered his arm so the gun was at his side.

Get rid of it, Jack.

My grandad opened the gun and took the bullets out, began wrapping the gun in the cloth again, carefully; put it back in the tin.

My grandad turned and came to the shed, looked at me like he'd forgotten I was there and put his hand on my head with the box in the other and said, Come on, darling, to me. He came back out of the shed and rinsed the whisky glasses at the outside tap and blinked in the sunlight like a mole. I mean like the mole when he emerges at the start of The Wind in the Willows. *I'd never seen a real mole. My grandad held his hand out to me for us to go back to the house, realized he still had the box that held the gun under his arm, which is how it ended up on the shelf in the garden shed. He swayed as he walked up the path. Freddie had his hand on my grandad's shoulder to steady him.*

A couple of times, the odd chance I've had when I could get into the shed on my own, I've stood on the little set of steps and checked to see the blue metal box at the back of the shelf. It's still there. I think my grandad was right to keep it. You never know, really, when we might need it.

'Rejoice.'

We get an old banger from Harry Robertson, a beaten-up Marina. It's brown, but the front driver's wing is grey. He gives it to my dad for free; well, for helping him with the cars. My dad sells his Cortina. I can see that my mum hates the new car. I like it. She's embarrassed of it outside our house. She doesn't want to be but she is. She looks at it out of the front window at Crow Street.

Where you gonna park it?

What dyer mean?

Where yer gonna park the car?

We've got a drive. On the drive.

My mum used to say she didn't care where she lived but she did. It was important to her what everyone else thought. It's human nature, I suppose. Later, she really didn't care what anyone thought, but that was later, and even then she did her drinking in the house, in her room. Even down Crow Street there were people who didn't know what was happening.

We never used to speak to the people in Elm Drive, except sometimes on Sunday mornings, when the men used to clean their cars. My dad didn't clean the Marina. My mum said if he tried to clean it, it would fall apart; it was only rust and dirt holding it together. I remember he smiled at her and didn't get angry.

The police stop us on a Sunday morning. We are turning, where Watson's Green Road goes up the hill by Green Park when the police car appears behind us and flashes its lights and pulls up in front of us. A policeman gets out of the car. I can see the fat shape of the other policeman, sitting in the driver's seat.

My dad winds down the window. The policeman knows his name.

Morning, Francis.

All right, my dad says. He keeps looking straight up the hill towards the flats, not at the policeman. I look at the policeman. I try and stare him out like Michael Campbell does to the teachers. They can't arrest me for staring. He doesn't look at me, just at my dad.

The policeman's head comes right in the car. If we wound the window up quickly we could chop his head off.

Where we off to then?

I'm driving home with my son. I've been to buy some paint.

This was true. We were going to paint the back door.

Okay to have a look in the boot, Francis? the policeman says.

My dad doesn't say anything, nods a little bit and opens his door. The policeman doesn't step back from the door like you'd expect, stands against it so there's a narrow gap for my dad to get out of. I want him to push the door open, smash the policeman in his balls. That would take the look off his face.

Just stay there, son. Okay? my dad says to me. We woh be a minute.

Well, that might depend, Francis, won't it? the policeman says.

The fat policeman, the driver, the same one again, gets out of the car and walks towards us.

Look, I've got me son with me.

We can see that, Francis.

We can see that.

Yer never know when we might want to speak to yer, mate.

We might want yer any time, mate. There's a lot we might want to speak to yer about. There's a lot of people we might want to speak to yer about.

Any time, Francis, any time.

The policemen are talking in quiet, friendly voices but you can tell they're not friendly at all. I know they mean Charlie Clancey. They want to talk about Charlie. His trial's coming up; I've heard my dad say.

My dad opens the boot for them. There is nothing in there. The tins of paint are by my feet because we didn't want them to roll around. The police stand and look at the empty boot.

Where's yer new car from, Francis? One of Harry's, is it?

It's weird, how the police know everyone we know.

My dad has to get the documents for our car and take them to the police car. They stand and talk some more. I can't hear them. My dad nods a couple of times. His eyes look at the pavement. I don't want to see him, looking like that. I've got my book with me, a guide to the World Cup. The captain of Honduras has recovered from smallpox. The capital city of Cameroon is Yaoundé. Poland's star player is called Zbigniew Boniek.

A game kicks off on the pitch at Green Park so I try to concentrate on that. A team in yellow goes on the attack. Their goalkeeper is smoking a cigarette.

My dad gets back to the car.

Okay, son, we can go home now, get that painting done.

I nod.

The goalkeeper's smoking, I say.

He looks at the pitch for a minute. The keeper stubs the cigarette out on the post.

Doh say nuthin about the police to yer mummy, eh?

I don't like it when he says mummy. It makes me feel like a little boy. I don't say anything about it, though. I can tell he's upset. His hand is shaking when he tries to put the key in the ignition.

Okay, I say.

The police wait in their car. Our car doesn't start first time, it never does; then when my dad does get it going we roll backwards up the kerb. The goalkeeper lets the ball through his hands and into the goal. As we drive up and past the police car I look at the policemen and try to stare them out. They are laughing.

Charlie went to prison, no one else. It didn't do anything to him, he was only in a couple of months and he'd been in before. Tommy came back to feed his horses and all work stopped. My dad did a few bits and pieces for Harry but the police didn't seem interested in that any more; they didn't come down Crow Street.

We settled into a routine then, with my dad and grandad at home. Johnny would get back from his work and go and sit down the end of the garden and paint the deserted allotments. Sunday mornings, or other times when there was no one around, he'd pull the fence back and go in there and have a wander around with his sketchbook. There were signs up about how dangerous it was, how the ground might cave in. He painted a toad he found sitting on one of the paths. He told me he thought we'd see snakes in there soon. The foxgloves grew higher than the sheds, then a sunflower appeared and he sat at the end of the garden with his feet up on the fence drawing the swirls of the sunflower and the crows that flew back and forth from Cinderheath.

Sometimes, if it was warm enough, Natalie would go down the end of the garden with Leah. She was learning to walk. I saw Johnny and Natalie holding hands across the fence one time, Leah toddling to the wall and back, laughing. Johnny finished a sunflower, tore the page from the book and handed it to Natalie.

What if I love her? Johnny says to my mum.
Well, thass great then, doh look so miserable about it!
No, but another bloke's babby, kid, I doh know.
Johnny stares across the kitchen. My mum touches his hand. I'm sitting with my back to the door, reading. They've forgotten I'm there.
But if you do love her, John?
I doh know.
If you do love her, that's a great thing, a lovely thing. And you do know. If you do love her, you do know.
But what if I cor trust her?
Johnny bites the skin around his fingers; my mum holds his other hand.
People make mistakes, Johnny, they do. I ay tellin yer it's great. It ay a very good situation, is it? But it does happen. It wor like you was together when it happened. I mean, her ay betrayed yer if thass what yer think.
Iss a big thing, though.

Of course it is. It's yer life.

They sit quietly for a bit. There is a saucepan boiling on the hob and the lid rattles, my mum goes and turns the gas down, opens the window a crack to get rid of the condensation.

Is he still around, the dad?

He ay no good.

That'll be hard.

If I did, if we did, then it'd have to be as if Leah was mine.

My mum nods and says, It'll still be hard.

I doh know.

I think yer know what yer should do. I doh mean I know; I mean deep down you know yerself.

Johnny nods.

I'll tell yer another thing, she says. If yer decide not to then that has to be it, you have to put it behind yer; one way or the other yow've gorra decide. Iss a big thing, Johnny, course it is.

I doh know, Johnny says and gets up to put the kettle on.

Pour us a drink, Johnny, will yer? My mum pushes a glass across the table.

Yer wanna watch what yome drinking, Johnny says.

Doh yow start as well. She taps the glass and says, This is the least of me worries.

There are piles of stuff at the house, photos, clothes, even a reel of old ciné film we took at the caravans once, Johnny's sketchbooks. I'll burn it all, I think, when it comes to it, not look at any of it, watch the ashes drift over the hill.

We sit and watch the World Cup together at my nan and grandad's, every game; Johnny rushes back from work to catch the end of the afternoon games. We go for day trips in the summer, not far: Worcester, Stratford, Evesham. My dad still points out the nice houses to my mum, in the countryside, and closer to home like on Oakham Road and by the Priory ruins, but now I know we'll never live in them. That suits me fine.

I started secondary school at Cinderheath that year; I got picked for the team, scored a goal from outside the box against Claughton with my dad and grandad watching. We got set a piece of homework to draw our dream house, the same as years before. I got Johnny to design a palace for me with swimming pools and hanging gardens and a horse-racing track with a grandstand; wrote my name on it when he'd finished. I wasn't making the same mistake twice. I got a certificate and a letter home to say how good my work was. Things went okay. I made new friends, one was a lad called Spencer O'Brien, we played in midfield together, although he moved away with his family not long after my dad died. His dad moved for work, to make nuclear submarines up in Barrow-in-Furness. There was a lot of that, then, moving if you got the chance.

The truth is that I had the time of my life for that year or so. It's one of the things I feel guilty about now, I suppose. It didn't last, it couldn't; the wave was towering above us about to crash down. Margaret Thatcher's voice was still playing in the background. God knows what lengths my mum was going to in order to show that things were fine and would be back on track at any minute, as soon as my dad got a new job. Then things took a turn for the much, much worse.

With Charlie, I hear my dad say.

Charlie has been out of prison for a couple of months now. He came round our house and my mum walked down the drive and told him to piss off, to never come near us again. He took ages trying to reverse his rag and bone van all down our road. My dad stayed inside. My mum stood on our drive, glaring at him.

Not after last time, my mum says to my dad. Yer need to get a proper job, Francis. Yow've stopped looking.

There ay no jobs.

Yer doh know if there's no jobs if yow ay lookin. When yer was first out of work yow was walking round places, asking around, waiting for the paper. Now, I doh know, Francis, I just doh know.

Who's gonna want me?

I doh know what yome talkin about.

Who's gonna have me now?

I doh know what we'm gonna do, Francis.

I doh know what we'm gonna do, my dad replies.

He stays in bed until late in the morning. My mum says he isn't very well, if people ask. I think he's okay. He's tired and worn out because of Margaret Thatcher. I understand. One teatime she is on the news and he looks up at her face and says, I doh know why somebody doh shoot that bitch.

On the days he stays in bed I go upstairs and read the paper to him when I come home from school. If it's a Thursday I leave it open at the jobs page. My mum reads the jobs to him as well, then she comes downstairs for her glass of wine, then gin, or both on some nights when it's not gone so well.

'Our history is the story of
a free people – a great chain
of people stretching back
into the past and forward
into the future.'

When Margaret Thatcher called a general election Johnny was good to his word and I helped him. We delivered Labour Party leaflets, round by us, all over Cinderheath for Jim Bayliss, the councillor, who Johnny knew through the football club. I'd do one side of the street and Johnny would do the other. On some of the nights after school, as the election got nearer, Jim let me go in the car with the speaker and let me talk into the microphone. I got to take turns with his nephew, Rob. He was a couple of years younger than me, a football prospect, Tom Catesby's son; he ended up at the Villa, then back at Cinderheath, years later. He runs the junior side there now. Robert Catesby: I thought his name was somehow a good omen.

Use your vote, use your vote wisely. Vote Labour, I'd say. Vote for Dr John Gilbert. Vote Labour.

I doh know how her thinks her's gonna win with all these millions unemployed. Two, three, fower; they'm lying about them figures, I'll tell yer that for nothing. I doh know nobody with a job. My grandad is talking over the telly and a report that says Margaret Thatcher is ahead in an opinion poll. It says people think she's doing the right things.

I've got a job, Dad, my mum says. She's even got a couple of extra hours' cleaning on a morning now.

I mean man's work, men's jobs.

And what abaht me? Johnny says.

Yer know what I mean.

My grandad never talks about Johnny as a real worker. I think he feels bad that Johnny has to work as hard as him, wishes he'd gone back to college, or that he'd not made him leave in the first place. Johnny looks at my grandad. Johnny stands up at the kitchen window. My grandad doesn't look at him.

I'm the onny one turning up any rent, after all, Johnny says and he looks at my grandad again and my grandad won't look at him, stares at the arm of the chair.

It's true that some people are going to vote Conservative. There are people in the big houses on Oakham Road with blue posters up. I've started writing their addresses down in a notebook in case we might need their names any time in the future. I told Jim Bayliss I'm doing it so we'd know where they lived as research for the election, so they don't do things like pretend they want a lift to the polling station and then go and vote Tory when they get there. That sort of thing happens all the time. I heard the men joking about it. Really, though, I'm writing their names down in case there's a revolution and we can send the police to their houses or stop them in their cars like the police did to my dad. You need this sort of information. I haven't told anyone that's my reason, though, not even Johnny. I know I have to pretend I want everything to be fair. I couldn't care less whether the election is fair or not. I just want to win and make sure that Margaret Thatcher isn't prime minister any *more. She can go and live in the Falkland Islands if she loves them that much.*

There are people who say to your face that they are going to vote Conservative. They're not all in the big houses, either. Some of them live round by my nan and grandad's.

A man shouts, Enoch was right, *after us down Juniper Close when I deliver a leaflet and he tries to set his Alsatian down the street after us but the Alsatian barks and then sniffs round the lamp-post. Enoch Powell is a big hero to them. Even he doesn't like Margaret Thatcher, though, so I don't know what their problem is.*

We might be disappointed by the election, Sean. Yer know that, don't yer?

What dyer mean?

Well, the Conservatives will probably win. Margaret Thatcher will still be prime minister. We'll carry on best we can. I don't want yer to worry about it so much. It's nice you're helping out but yome thirteen years old, darling. I doh want yer to worry so much. Maybe I shouldn't have let yer go and help em. Why doh yer ask Michelle what her's doing at the weekend? You've been happier lately; less look forward to summer. Doh worry about the election.

We'll win, I say, we'll win.

We didn't. The people loved Margaret Thatcher. They loved her, wanted her to be prime minister for ever, some of them, anyway. They loved other people being put out of work; they loved the factories closing; they loved rich people being rich; they loved the royal family and the House of Lords and the Empire; they loved Britannia ruling the waves; they loved going to war; they loved other people being poor and sick; they loved selling everything off to rich people to make them richer; worse, selling stuff that we already owned back to us. They loved rubbing our noses in the dirt. That's what they wanted and that's what they got.

Voting was meant to be fair. I decided right then, that night, when I was allowed to stay up to watch the results with my mum; that voting wasn't fair at all. My dad had stayed in bed, he had voted, though, and there was no worry about who he'd voted for this time. We would have to do something else to get rid of her.

If you were going to kill her, when would you do it? I ask Johnny. He laughs and then thinks about it.

Well, I doh know, he says, cleaning his football boots on the back step. That's a good question. If you think about successful assassinations, like Abraham Lincoln and the Kennedys, well, iss usually when they'm in a vulnerable position. Lincoln was in the theatre, relaxing, Bobby Kennedy was in the kitchen of a hotel, yer know; yer have to get em when their guard's down or they're somewhere they wouldn't be usually, right through history. So I'd go for either somewhere where she felt really safe, or a time when she was in the open and really vulnerable and weak. Maybe when her's on holiday or summat. Then he laughed a little bit more. I doh know if her goes on holiday. I'm sure there's plenty of people thinking about it right now.

I'm thinking about it, I say.

He laughs again and says, And me, our kid, in a voice like my grandad's.

I think, No, I really am thinking about it. I know where there's a gun.

Doh worry abaht it, Sean. It'll be all right. We'll all be all right.

We weren't all right, though, were we?

I've left my maths book at home. We have a test tomorrow. It's the end-of-year test, to sort out the classes for September. I have to do well to get into the top group so I can show my mum and dad that I'm working hard. It makes them feel better. I'm not thinking about the gun. I'm not thinking about Margaret Thatcher. No one cares anyway. Everything has carried on. I ask Michelle one break-time whether she saw the election.

What yer bothered about that shit for? she says and then asks me if I like her nail varnish. It's silver.

Yeah, I say, yeah, iss nice. Better than them gloves with no fingers.

What?

Yer looked like summat out of Thriller.

She whacks me on the shoulder but laughs and things feel all right.

I knew there was something wrong when I got to the house. I'd never liked it; it was like it was never really our house, not at all, and that we'd bought it, or were buying it, but it would never really be ours. I don't know why they didn't give it up earlier. I don't know why they kept on scraping the money together, borrowing more somehow, whatever. It was the reason my dad went back to work for Charlie when he got things together again after coming out of prison, the reason my dad started getting out of bed in the morning.

I thought of the ghosts of the trees out the back and the branches leaning towards the windows like Margaret Thatcher's fingers reaching out to get us. Unlike my nan and grandad's house, which really did belong to us, all of us, and to my great-granny and my great-grandad before us, who I'd only ever seen in a tiny sepia photograph dressed in uniform for some war or other, that was in a drawer in the sideboard and is still there today. Maybe I'll save some of the photos from the bonfire, stick them up on the wall of the pub. People love that kind of stuff, after all. How we used to live. We was poor but happy. Don't think for one minute that's what I'm saying, though.

I own that house now. I bought it with the pub takings, cash. Not that we had to pay much for it.

Margaret Thatcher would be proud.

It belonged to the council, but that meant it belonged to all of us, everyone had a share. And when we were dead and gone someone else would have it. That was how it was meant to work.

From each according to his ability, to each according to his need, that's what my grandad would say, even though he'd then spend an hour telling Johnny that if he thought things were ever going to change for the better he had another thing coming. That's what I was thinking about, the house, at least that's what I remember. I might have been thinking about Michelle's silver nail varnish and whether I'd get to walk home with her after the test or whether Rodney James would be hanging around to see her, when I came through the door and saw the handprint of blood on the banister rail.

I can hear the sound of something dripping, a very faint drip, drip, drip, and I think how you never get sounds like that in our house where everything is new and quiet, not like at my nan and grandad's, where there's always a tap dripping or the pipes bursting in the winter if you're not careful, and the sounds of the plumbing from all the other houses in the row. There's just this drip, drip, drip and everything is icy cold.

I went cold, I remember that. And I remember I said hello and I might have even called out *Dad?* even before I saw him, because who else could have been in the house? I knew where everyone else was and I'd just left my mum and I was old enough, too old, to believe in monsters and ghosts, although I still liked to tell myself I did. It was only later that I realized that the monsters and ghosts existed all along, whether I believed in them or not.

There is blood in a puddle on the chair by the phone, the phone is off the hook, the mouthpiece dropped on the floor with a handprint like on the banister, and there's blood on the stair carpet and on the walls on the way up.

I remember thinking that the blood had made the same patterns as the shit that Jermaine had smeared on the toilet walls back at primary school.

Drip, drip, drip. The bathroom door is open and as I turn at the top of the stairs I can see the water pooling inside the door and the metal floor strip is holding the puddle of water back from coming out onto the carpet and the water is pink. There's a pool of water with swirls of red in it and I'm looking at that and then look up so I can see through the half-open door and there's my dad sitting underneath the sink, leaning against the bath. His chest and head are turned towards me and his arm is dangling over the edge of the bath.

The sink tap is running. Harry's shirt is blocking the plughole. I know it's Harry's. I saw him fixing cars in it last night. Light blue, short sleeves, with oil stains where he's wiped his hands. Water comes over the sink's brim, drip, drip, drip. My dad is grey. His eyes look at me but he can't see anything and his mouth is open and I can see his teeth and it's like he's empty. He's not here. There's blood in his lap. There are more red handprints along the bath, on the edge of the sink, on the door. I stand there and look at him, can't move, stand looking and looking. There's blood. His eyes look like pearls. I know he's dead. I stand here for a long time, I can't move. They killed him. They killed him.

After a while I turn and I walk into my room and get my maths book and then I run down the stairs and out of the front door and up the hill all the way back to my mum and my nan and grandad and I can't speak when I get there, can't cry or shout or say anything, but I know straight away they can see something terrible has happened. My grandad jumps in one of Harry's cars, one that goes, so it's him who gets there first and sees exactly the same thing as me and he phones for the ambulance and probably the police, they come too now, and he does it so my mum doesn't have to see what me and my grandad have seen.

I think my grandad shut the door and maybe he shut my dad's eyes and mouth too, but I remember my mum screaming, just screaming. And I thought, They killed him, and I still hadn't made a sound, but I do remember thinking that one day I would do something to the people who'd killed my dad, that I would do something to get our revenge.

I never went in that house ever again. We stayed at my nan and grandad's and my mum fetched my things for me. I wished they could blow it up like they had my dad's other house, blow it all up like Quarry End. We couldn't have gone on living there anyway because we'd run out of money and the building society was about to take the house back. It didn't matter who owned the house. It had caused more trouble than it was worth, that was what my grandad said in the first place, like a curse, and he was right.

They rode around with him bleeding to death in the back of the car for an hour, keeping away from the police. I got all this from Charlie years later, and I think he was telling the truth, even though he didn't usually. They didn't talk about any of this at the trial. There was something the police had done wrong so they adjusted all the times to make it look like they'd chased them straight from the factory to our house. It wasn't like that at all, though. It meant Charlie and the others weren't charged with anything to do with my dad, only with stealing. The police didn't want to get themselves into trouble and Charlie told his solicitor to accept the police's version of the events even though you could see that the times didn't add up. Charlie reckoned it might mean a shorter sentence for him. He told me that when they first took them to the police station and put him in the cells, an officer he'd never seen before, with a smart suit on, not a uniform, serious crime squad, Charlie thought, came to the door and whispered that my dad was dead and that him and his mates were all going to get charged with murder. Charlie told me that just then he didn't care because he felt so bad about my dad, if the police weren't lying and it was true he was dead, and that he felt that he had killed my dad, in a way. He said that he'd sat on the edge of the cell bed rocking back and forth, whereas usually he'd sit there like he wasn't bothered, which he wasn't normally. Prison didn't do anything to him. He wasn't a murderer, though.

You didn't kill him, Charlie, I said to him on the night he told me all this.

I did, son, in a way. I just wish we'd gone to the hospital straight away or gid up instead of running. I wish that every day.

I don't think he could believe I was sitting there talking to him about it. He kept glancing up at the bar door, which had the bolt across, but only one. I think he weighed up whether he could beat me to the door or not, but there was no way. He resigned himself, I think, slumped down in the chair, went for confession, contrition. A lot of it was true, I think. He meant what he said. He couldn't make me out. I think he didn't understand why I didn't want to kill him. By that time I'd had enough of wanting to kill people. This was fifteen years later, after I came back, after my mum died.

You didn't kill him, Charlie. Yer day kill him.

I wish I'd done summat different.

I know. Yer day kill him, Charlie. Someone else killed him. Something else did.

He looked at me. He had no idea what I was talking about. His hands were shaking and I poured him a drink.

They rode around with him bleeding to death for an hour,

keeping away from the police. They didn't know he was bleeding to death. He said he was okay, not great, keep the towel pressed to his leg, he'd be okay. They'd been disturbed shifting the parts from a machine at a plastics place that hadn't long closed over off Greets Green. My dad was on top of the machine when the police arrived, he slipped and fell onto the blade he was trying to remove. Harry pulled him up off the blade and helped him run to the car. It hadn't seemed that bad. He'd run, held up by Harry, his hand pressed to the wound, and they'd got in the back of the car. The police were at one end of the factory but the car was at the other so they got away. The police had to drive out onto the industrial estate and back around, in a loop of the building, which meant Charlie could pull out onto the main road. They could get away, they thought. Charlie's mind was already racing. He'd burn the car out in the field behind his house. It was a piece of shit anyway. They could hear the police siren.

He needs the hospital, Charlie. Harry said.

I'm all right, I'm all right, my dad said.

There's blood gooin everywhere.

Harry was beginning to panic. Charlie turned to have a look: my dad's legs were across Harry's lap, bleeding into it and the seat, but then he took the car up the kerb and nearly into a lamp-post.

Hold summat on it, he said. There's a towel on the floor somewhere.

Tommy was in the passenger seat. Charlie never usually took him with them but he'd stayed when Charlie was in prison, even remembered to feed the horses. He was pissed, no use to anyone. Charlie was cursing bringing him, now.

Just hold summat on it.

That helped, stopped the blood coming so strong.

Tight as yer can, thass it, Charlie said.

My dad was breathing through his teeth.

I'm all right, he said, all right. Less get out of here.

Tie summat round his leg, Ron, above the cut. Stop it coming as much.

Harry ripped his shirt, wrapped it round my dad's thigh above where he was holding the towel. The towel felt hot.

Thass it, thass it.

I'm all right, my dad said. I'm all right.

They rode around West Bromwich for an hour with him bleeding to death, looking out for police cars, the sounds of sirens around every corner.

We need the hospital, Harry said. We could go to Hallam, up there, Sandwell Hospital.

I'm tougher than I look, my dad said as a joke.

They tried to go to the hospital. Charlie said they rode past twice in ten minutes. The first time there was a police car parked at the entrance to Casualty. The second time, as he slowed down, they saw the flashing lights in the rear-view mirror, heard a siren and got scared and drove off again. They talked about dumping him on the pavement outside.

I'm all right, I'm all right, my dad kept saying.

Harry wanted to get on the motorway, drive down to Kidderminster, up to Walsall, drop him at a hospital there, dump the car, get the train back, walk back, for Christ's sake.

Just get me home. I'm all right. I'm all right. I can get a bandage on in the house. I'm all right.

They got him back, driving around, back roads, thought they'd done it, got away. Charlie turned the car around on the drive, backed right up and Harry helped my dad through the front door. Harry sat my dad on the chair by the telephone, told him to phone for an ambulance, told him to say he'd fallen off a step-ladder doing a bit of decorating, something like that. He left him on the chair with the phone in his hand, he said. He hadn't dialled it for him, could hear the sirens and panicked.

They got pulled over around the corner from our house, in the bus stop. The police asked why there was blood all over the seat, all over Harry with no shirt on. They didn't answer. Tommy told a policeman to fuck off. They punched him in the balls and got him in the van, he threw up on the policeman's shoes. He threw up everywhere and the policeman punched him again. Off they went to the station. If I'd looked up when I got to the corner of the road, I'd have seen the car, listing into the bus stop, a police motorbike parked alongside it, waiting for a wagon to come and pick it up.

The day of the funeral is hot and bright. We should have been thinking about the caravans, the sunlight on the sea. The funeral car drives past the shops by the Pig on the Wall on the way to the crematorium. All the boys there have got their shirts off, lying in the sun eating ice lollies. I see two lads from football. One of them, David Harvey, has transferred a tattoo from a comic on his shoulder. It's the Incredible Hulk. David laughs at something Jason Kelly says to him. Jay plays up front and all the girls fancy him. His ear-ring glints in the sun and I think, My dad's dead, and we drive right by them and they don't look. They wouldn't look up at a funeral car, not boys my age, eating ice lollies, messing about with cartoon tattoos, and I think, I am the same as them, but I am looking at them through the glass, wearing an itchy suit in mourning for my dad I want right now, more than anything, to be sitting there by the shops at the Pig on the Wall, where the people put the pig up on the wall to watch the band go by, that was the story; to be happy, to be laughing there in the sunshine, laughing about some silly joke or noise, being happy. And my dad to be alive.

We went back to my nan and grandad's. I remember my mum holding me and crying, saying how we had to look after each other now that it was only the two of us and that we'd make sure to look after each other. But we didn't. We didn't do a very good job of that at all.

I'm silent. There's nothing to say. Sometimes at school they get people to come in and talk to me about it, like that's going to help, talking to a stranger, like that's going to bring him back. There are two of them. They come at different times. One of them says she's an educational psychologist. I don't know who the other one is, maybe a government agent come to kill me too, a Tonton Macoute straight from Margaret Thatcher's skeleton army. They try to get me to draw pictures to show how I feel. They can see how I feel. They don't need a bloody picture. I can't draw. I should get Johnny to do it for me. Talking to them about it isn't going to make me feel any better.

I wasn't stupid. I didn't think government agents had broken into the house and killed him, of course I didn't. We knew what had happened, although I didn't know the details until later. I used to look up at the castle battlements and wait for his ghost to appear. I'd talk to him, tell him that something was rotten, all right, the whole country, top to bottom.

I want to say to them that you helped kill him, coming here and nodding your heads and looking like you care, when really you turn up in your cars from wherever your offices are and go through the motions and shake your heads and say what a shame and get paid for it, like that's a proper job, not making anything or doing anything, writing reports saying this boy is very sad and angry because his dad's dead, and his family has lost his house, his mum's started drinking, his world has been blown to bits.

Michelle says she's sorry about my dad and gives me a hug. Then she goes to watch Jaws *at the pictures with Rodney James.*

'We always have to be
aware of the enemy within,
which is much more
difficult to fight and more
dangerous to liberty.'

I sit on buses, not going to school, not going anywhere, there and back, fourteen years old, reading Orwell on the top deck, dreaming. I take the books from Johnny's bookshelf, get others from the library. It is 1984. I read 1984 over and over, Thatcher's boot stamping on our face for ever, Homage to Catalonia, Down and Out . . ., The Road to Wigan Pier. *He missed a trick there. I got a book from the library that had Orwell's diary at the beginning of the Wigan Pier journey. He started in Birmingham, went to Stourbridge, Wolverhampton, skirted us somehow, like Queen Victoria. Dudley Port: Wigan Pier.*

Shouldn't yer be at school, son?

On strike.

Who? Yow or the taychers?

The bus drivers nod when I get on, don't say much. I look at the blue patterns tattooed on their bare arms, the heater on in the cab. I like the number 74 best, or the 120. So I sit in traffic at Dudley Port or on Soho Road and Winston Smith scribbles away in the corner of his room; or we'll be outside Thimblemill Baths or at the level crossing by the Langley Maltings and a sniper fires down the Ramblas, crack, crack, crack. By the twisted pipes, rising above the wall at Albright & Wilson, O'Brien explains how I will come to love Big Brother.

I could've gone anywhere, within reason, off to the countryside at least, Clent, Kinver, got the bus to Stourbridge and then out to Stourport or somewhere. If I'd left early enough on a morning I could have ridden the train all the way to Machynlleth, Aberystwyth, Porthmadog, back again, dodged the fares, it was easy, looked at hills and mountains, waterfalls. I could've gone for good, disappeared, got on my bike like Tebbit told us to. I never did, though. I made for the ruins. Last factories, red bricks gone black from soot, stained concrete, smashed glass, rust everywhere. On the railway bridge over Tipton Road someone had written: MY NAME IS OZYMANDIAS, KING OF KINGS.

Yer need to watch him, Dad.

How dyer expect him to be with what's happened?

I doh expect nothing. I'm just saying we've gorra keep an eye on him. I cor if I ay back from work till now.

Johnny is talking to my grandad at the kitchen table. They think I'm upstairs but I came down to get a biscuit.

I just think, how dyer expect him to be? He's all right. In the circumstances.

Watch him, thass what I say.

What dyer think he's gonna do?

Johnny doesn't reply straight away. Through the gap in the door I can see him dipping bread in his gravy. My grandad looks at him, not like he used to, waiting for him to say something stupid. He wants him to say something that makes sense. Johnny shrugs.

I doh know. All I'm saying is we need to keep an eye on him. Iss common sense, really. We need to watch him.

I ride on buses or sit in the library. I have to wait until the afternoon for the library because the women there phone school if they think you're skiving off. Skiving off to learn things. I'm doing research, I say. I am. I turn a school exercise book I've never written in into my assassination journal. I sit in the library and think about Catesby, how his gunpowder plot failed because too many people got involved. There are traitors everywhere.

I daydream revolution. The royal family will go off in exile. We don't have to kill everyone but we'll release people from prison and put the people who have caused all the problems in there instead. We'll have trials. We'll put Margaret Thatcher on trial and we'll have all sorts of people giving evidence to prove what she's done and she'll be found guilty and sentenced to death. And everyone will want to see it, like we'll have to think about doing it on a Saturday afternoon at Wembley so it'll be like the cup final or maybe we'll chop her head off in Trafalgar Square and let people celebrate in the fountains like on New Year's Eve. We could take her head around the country on a spike on the back of a van so people can see that she's really dead, although maybe that's too much. We don't want a reign of terror. The killing will have to stop, although there are a lot of people asking for it. Maybe we'll handle it really carefully and she'll be shot somewhere in a prison yard early in the morning without much notice and we'll do a little announcement on the news: Margaret Thatcher was killed early this morning. All factories that have been closed will open again on Monday, all mines, all shipyards, all docks, open as usual. Please report to work as normal.

I will raise my dad from the dead.

*

I know where there's a gun.

I go to the library every day, think about how to do it, scribble plans in a code in my exercise book. I read the papers. I look at maps. I ride my bike and ride on buses. I want something that will work. You can forget things like the opening of parliament. I don't want symbols. I'm not Catesby. I want something that will work. I am the enemy within.

She was our enemy within.

Her body. We'll have to do something with it, dump it somewhere, burn it maybe. There will be people who will still be on her side.

Leave her for the bastard crows, my grandad said when he heard them talking about the possibility of a state funeral.

I take the gun from the shed. I feel for it at the back of the shelf and there it is: a blue tin box with an old gun inside it. I put the newspapers back in the box, along with the message I've written, and then I take the gun out and put it in my bag.

I ride my bike up to the quarries; the bike that had been Eric's that I am big enough for now. I go all the way to Quarry End, up to the ridge of ash trees on the lip of the quarry, watch the light dim and the men in the quarry as they park up the diggers and chain them together and go clumping up the path in their boots to clock out. When they've gone and it's almost dark I creep past all the signs, more signs, saying DANGER *and then* DANGER OF DEATH. *I think, oh there's that, all right. There's danger at every* turn. I look for a guard. It's a new job for people, guarding places that are empty, to stop people like Charlie and my dad taking the stuff, but there is no guard here.

I have a torch and I walk to the middle of the quarry, tell myself I'm at the spot where my dad was born, out past the diggers that are still now in the half-light and look like giraffes paused at a drinking hole and I put the greasy bullets into the chamber. It's true that my grandad must've cleaned the gun. I can sense it will work. It's heavy in my hand. I hold it out in front of me with two hands like in Starsky and Hutch and I point it at the wall of rock in the distance. I squeeze the trigger, gently at first, because that's how I've read you do it, and then, just as I think it's no good, maybe it won't work, maybe I'll go home and stop all this, it goes off with a crash and throws my hands up above my head. I almost topple over, stumble backwards and the shot echoes and echoes. The roar stays in my ears and I pick up my bag and run. I scamper through the last of the light, the scree giving way on this shallow side of the quarry and think I must have woken the whole of Dudley with the explosion, my ears still ringing and hurting, my arms and body aching from the impact.

Then, from the corner of my eye, there it is, the grey fox slinking up and off the path in front of me, into the trees, maybe the son or daughter of the one I'd seen with my dad right here, when it had been a road, a row of houses, here where we had lit the bonfire of all that furniture. All of it gone: the house, the road, the people, their things, like they had never been here at all.

I throw up when I get to the cover of the trees, being careful not to be sick on the gun. The gun is hot. I turn the torch on to check it and then lie on the soft grass at the *edge of the quarry to listen to sounds on the road. Lights are coming on in the houses. I walk out of the shadows and head home for tea feeling about ten foot tall. I think about the man they chased down into the quarry all those years ago. I swagger with the gun in my bag. I'm going to do this. My nan has cooked sausages. She looks after me now. My mum sits in the chair, with my nan watching her drink, saying she can't go on like this. I don't know what to say to her. I put my clothes in the bag on top of the gun and put it under my bed.*

The next morning I got on my bike, pretended to leave for school, like I did every day, sometimes going to school, most often not. I'd taken some cash from the back of my mum's bedside cabinet, where she tucked the odd note away to buy bottles of gin with. I freewheeled down the hill to Dudley Port station and bought a ticket to Birmingham, chained my bike to the railings, and waited for the train. When I got to Birmingham I bought a ticket to London and from London on to Brighton. I remember the feeling of riding down the hill, the gun heavy in the bag. I felt free. If I ever had to talk about it to anyone now I'd probably say, Oh, I didn't know what I was doing, all that stuff you hear. That morning as I rode down the hill I knew exactly what I was doing.

I'd imagined riding all the way there, sleeping in fields, barns, ditches at the side of the road. It would become part of the legend after I'd killed her. People would talk about glimpsing me on the route. A girl in Oxfordshire would remember taking apples to a strange boy who had crept into her father's barn; taking him apples and lying him down on the straw. People would follow the route like a pilgrimage: Dudley, Stratford, Chipping Norton, Abingdon, Aldershot, English places, to the soft slope of the Downs and England's descent into the sea.

They were in Brighton for their conference, their victory rally.

I watched the country as the train slipped through it, a patchwork of autumn green and brown. Once you left Birmingham not much of it looked like it did where we lived. It made me think. I wondered if what I was doing was for the whole country and whether they'd thank me. Who was I kidding? What I was doing was for me. The bag on my lap, I would put my hand inside and on the gun for reassurance. I looked out across the green and brown of the hills and fields.

I sit on the pebbles and look at the piers, the one with the glowing lights off to my left and the ruined one in front of me. The metal makes criss-crosses against the white band of sky behind it, between the grey clouds and the grey sea. It looks like the gantry at Cinderheath. It looks like an abandoned city, out there in the sea, like Atlantis, like Dudley Castle jutting out of its ocean of dead trilobites and dead factories.

I think I might have realized then, sitting there on the beach, that it was gone. I could kill her, but it wouldn't change anything. Nothing would come back.

I sit on the beach for a long time, watch it get dark. I move my legs on the pebbles and I push my back against the sea wall. The beach is different here from the one in Wales. We're not going to Wales again.

*It's bigger, busier, the beach here, even with no one out
there. I can feel the rumble of cars against my back through
the sea wall and hear the tyres as they swish along the
wet road. There's an orange fishing net laid out and held
down by rocks next to a few boats. A fat seagull sits and
pecks the edge of the net and another one sits in the boat.
Others are out on the sea watching it get dark like I am.
They are the kings here. There are big ships out near the
horizon. I think about them going off to America, Russia;
think maybe I could keep going, get on a boat and head off
to sea. But I don't really know how you do that and the
ships don't stop here. My bravery is disappearing, leaking
out of me onto the beach, into the sea. I am fourteen years
old, only a boy. I want my mum to be okay, my dad back.
Thoughts slap against me like the waves on the shingle.
The rhythm of the traffic against my back and the shush-
ing of the waves make me close my eyes. Maybe I could
sleep here. I hold the gun inside my bag to keep me warm.*

*I wake up, soaked through by a giant wave, swallowed
by the tide. I jolt upright in panic, soaking wet and
scared that I might drown, be swept away, but the sea
is still. The sound I heard, of the wave crashing into
the beach, of a giant wave to end it all, echoes through
the darkness, not only in my head, but in the damp sea
wall behind me. It comes through the air now like the
sound of shingle being torn off the beach. Then come
the shouts, people, and seagulls screaming. I am freezing
and I dig my fingers into the tops of my legs to try to
get them both to work. I can smell burning, taste dust,
ruin. It's not a seaside smell at all, it's something else, like
the taste of the ash that day with my dad up at Quarry*

End, burning everything that was left in the house he grew up in. Sirens start, there's more shouting. I get my legs going and wobble out of my little hollow and across the shifting pebbles.

The hotel has fallen down. That's what I can see. Or more, it's like the front has fallen off so all the layers that made it look like a cake have landed on top of each other. I keep my hand on the sea-wall rail and walk towards it. My heart is thumping. There is grit and dust in the sea air, in my eyes, making them water and blink. I'm scared. I've been scared for a long time. There are people where the hotel has fallen down. I hear voices, groaning, crying. I heard my great-granny once when they moved her downstairs, crying out in this deep moan, right near the end, like nothing I'd ever heard before except maybe from my mum when she heard what had happened to my dad. I can hear it now, in among the people, running now, and calling out to each other, and the sirens starting, flashing lights. I cling to the rail and listen to the sound, underneath it all, mixed with the grit and the dust, the argh, argh, argh sound, not words. There's shouting and running and tyres swooshing down to the hotel and police radios crackling and ambulance doors clattering open.

It's a bomb. Somebody has blown the hotel up. I can hear people say it's a bomb, and it is, hotels don't just fall down.

She has to get out of there, I know that. If she's alive, they'll get her out. If she's alive, she won't come out the front of the building. There's rubble and dust where the front doors are, fire engines and ambulances parked at angles. I walk along the front. Sirens echo like the gunshot in the quarry. There's a little side road that leads round to some doors. I'd seen them earlier when I walked round, *eating a bag of chips, doing reconnaissance. That's what it's called when you check on the place where you might kill someone. There are more cars parked here, police this time, more lights flashing.*

And there she is, in front of me. My hand is on the gun and I keep walking towards her. There are bodyguards, SAS, Tonton Macoute, but I don't look at them. There's Denis, with a suit on over his pyjamas, blinking. I look at her and then her eyes meet mine for a moment, that split second, her eyes bright and alert and a look of what, recognition, briefly, that is what it feels like, that she knows I'm coming, my hand on the gun, the gun still inside the bag, and this is it, this is the moment right now I think, and BANG, can't miss, and I step out of the shadows and then she passes, and she starts talking to a policeman and my hand is still in the bag holding the gun and they've gone past and I don't move and I see a policeman look over and then another turn his head and I swear for a moment they are the ones from Dudley, who came to speak to my grandad, who brought me and Ronnie home, who questioned my dad. I think, Oh no, here it goes, my hand still on the gun, inside the bag, and I turn and walk back into the shadows, and there is no hand on my shoulder, no shout or sirens for me, and I walk back out of history, and back around into the grim, dusty, bomb-blasted morning and stand there on the front. I can't get my breath. A woman, bleeding from the head, comes walking past me. I touch her arm, give her the towel that I'd packed on top of the gun.

Thank you, she says. Thank you.

I move away, away, lean on the railings, move back and back again, away from here, and then I see the policeman's face again, the same one who had been next to Margaret Thatcher, and so I keep walking. I don't know where I am going. There are people on stretchers, lights flashing. There are shouts and the caw of birds. People are dead, dying. I have the gun in my hand, my bag. I see her face, her eyes. I keep walking. I don't know what to do.

The sun rises behind me and as I walk along the front, past the abandoned pier, I see Johnny. And he grabs me, wraps his arms around me and picks me up off my feet and I'm not surprised; of course Johnny's here, anything is possible. I ask him if my dad is with him and he grabs me and I remember, no, my dad is dead. As Johnny holds me, by the grey and dirty English Channel, I decide I don't want to kill anyone; I don't want to kill anyone at all.

'You hear about these atrocities, these bombs but you don't expect them to happen to you. But life must go on as usual.'

I tode yer. I've bin tellin yer if yer would've listened.

This is what Johnny said to my grandad when he got back from work and they realized I had gone.

All right, son.

No, it ay all right, is it? I tode yer to watch him.

All right.

My nan came in from going up and down the street to see if anyone had seen me. She'd knocked at Paul and his mum's flat. Paul had told them he hadn't seen me at school since the start of term, sometimes I'd come to get my mark then get off over the fence, he hadn't seen me for months really.

I tode yer to watch him.

Okay. I'm sorry.

My mum sat rocking in the chair, her arms hugging herself, a bunch of screwed up tissue in one hand, not really saying anything.

They checked the shed. That was when my grandad reached up for the box at the back of the shelf and found my assassination statement folded neatly in the space where the gun should have been.

Johnny got the train. He saw the bike chained to the railings. My grandad had said he'd drive, would get a car off Harry, but when they looked out into the street they decided none of the cars would make it. They talked about phoning the police. Johnny got the last train into Brighton, slept on a bench until the bomb and the chaos that followed woke him up. He'd walked the streets, same as me, trying to stay close to the hotel, but far enough away not to get noticed by the police, wondering where I was, what I'd done.

We go to a café and watch the news and eat bacon and eggs. I'm starving. It's the best food I've ever tasted, shivering, my shoes off, resting my feet on a big heating pipe as Johnny goes to the phone at the back of the café. I can see him looking now, to check I'm not going to run off. I'm not going anywhere. Everybody's eyes are on the television set apart from Johnny looking at me. They keep showing Norman Tebbit coming out on a stretcher. There are people dead. They're not sure how many yet. The sun is shining.
  Where's the gun? Johnny says quietly.
  In the bag, I say.
  Okay, keep it there. You haven't fired it?
  Onny at the quarry. I fired it at the quarry. For practice.
  Fuckin hell.
  To check it worked.
  He looks at me.
  Where did you sleep?
  On the beach.
  You tired?
  I nod.
  It wouldn't do any good, would it? I say.
  No.
  Shooting anyone, I mean.
  No.

There's a big ship out on the sea, white spray at the prow as it moves slowly on.

Where's the letter I wrote?

In my pocket, he says.

I doh wanna kill nobody.

Good. That's good, Sean.

We can throw the letter away, in the sea or summat. I doh think all that now.

Okay, he says. I'm sorry, Sean, about everything.

Me too, I say. I don't want to kill anyone.

On the screen, Margaret Thatcher walks into the conference hall. It's down the road from where we're sitting. All the people are on their feet. Some workmen in the corner of the café start to clap. They clap and cheer in the hall as Margaret Thatcher gets to the podium, they wave their Union Jacks. They love her. She will be prime minister for ever. They've won. They'd have won if the bomb had blown her to kingdom come, if I'd shot her when I had the chance. They've won and there's nothing I can do about it. It isn't going to bring my dad back. It isn't going to bring anything back. She'll be there for ever.

'The fact that we are gathered here now – shocked but composed and determined – is a sign not only that this attack has failed but that all attempts to destroy democracy will fail.'

We stayed with Ronnie and his mum and sisters that night. Johnny had got the address from Natalie before he dashed for the train. They lived in a caravan park outside Worthing. Vanessa, Ronnie's mum, had taken up with the caretaker of the site. Ronnie woke up every day looking out at the sea. He didn't go to school much, like me. He helped out with odd jobs. People lived on the site in the winter while they looked for work; families who'd lost their houses or were on the run from something. There was a lot of that then, the whole country on their bike. I noticed the Man United Subbuteo team all standing up in a basket his mum had planted outside the caravan door.

Ronnie stayed down there, though his mum and sisters moved on over the years. He ended up caretaker of the site. We've been to visit a few times. The kids wake up in the caravan, gaze out at the sea; we walk down to the rock pools to look for crabs.

Johnny got the sack for not turning up for work. He tried to talk to his gaffer but it was no good. They were looking to get rid of people anyway. My grandad said he should go back to college. Johnny said it was too late now, and so he drifted in and out of work over the years.

My mum died. I couldn't help her, didn't help her. She went a few months after I came home in 1997. I should've done more sooner. By the time I came home there really was nothing to do. My nan sat with her every day, held her hand, sometimes lifted her drink to her lips, told her everything was all right. My nan and grandad dealt with it all at the end.

'I willingly grant the influence of free market economists, like Friedrich von Hayek and Milton Friedman. But the root of the approach we pursued in the 1980s lay deep in human nature, and more especially the nature of the British people.'

Johnny's still here, the same; he's past fifty now, thirty-odd years in and out of work; in and out of something with Natalie. He helped her through the years with Leah; helped Leah as much as he could. There's been no one else for either of them. I don't know why they didn't get together properly. Michelle tried to talk to him about it once but got nowhere. Maybe he still paints her sometimes. I saw him the other day, getting off the bus with Natalie, carrying her bags of shopping. She was leaning into him in the wind. He stood on the pavement edge like it was a clifftop, waiting for a gap in the traffic, equal parts timid and brave.

Johnny's not the only one. You see them here all the time, lost boys, men. I'd put him on the payroll but he prefers it this way now. He collects glasses, waits on tables, changes the odd barrel. I slip him a few notes from the till on a Friday afternoon. They send him on courses every now and again to try to get him into work, threaten to stop the little money he gets. He scrapes it together for a couple of pints and a game of snooker on odd afternoons, sits endlessly watching the news and bickering with my grandad. My nan died too, a few years ago, in her sleep, just past her eightieth birthday. No one killed her.

I help my grandad, eighty-nine now, down the steps of the pub and into the taxi and back to Crow Street. It's no place to live these days, but they carry on, my grandad and Johnny; Natalie and Harry. Someone underpinned the allotments, built new flats on the narrow strip of land there.

That world I grew up in has gone, transformed, but there are traces that remain; this pub and these streets; a cenotaph.

I hose down the concrete in front of the cellar doors. The draymen have been, like every Thursday, and left a trail of beer from the empty barrels, that goes sticky like blood on the pub yard. Charlie Clancey chimes the bell to get some service in the bar. He still brings his black wagon out and goes clip-clopping past the pub before he comes in for fish and chips; sometimes I take his money and sometimes I don't. In a minute, I will go and pour him half a mild, wait for Johnny and my grandad to come in for their dinnertime pint, wait for my grandad to ask me to put the news on the television and then wait for him to ask me to turn it off. As it's a Thursday we might get Harry too; Natalie brings him in near the end of the week if his legs are good enough. Michelle will come back from the day centre; she still does the odd shift there, although I tell her we don't need the money any more even though we do, holding the hands and wiping the snot from kids who can't look after themselves, and then she'll start the menu for the weekend, collect our own kids from school. Josh has got football tonight; Lily has dance class.

The sun catches the drops of water held in a spider's web woven in the old brickwork in the corner of the yard. The web trembles with the weight of the water but doesn't break. And for all I've said that I didn't want to kill anyone, I wonder if I did the right thing after all. I can't say there aren't days when I wish I'd just pulled the trigger.

Quotations from Margaret Thatcher

The words of Margaret Thatcher used in this novel come from the following sources:

20 February 1975, speech accepting the Conservative Party Leadership (p. 15); 4 May 1979, remarks on the Conservative Party election victory (p. 25); 20 September 1981, *News of the World* (p. 33); 2 May 1979, *Sun* (p. 43); 14 May 1981, letter to United States Senators Kennedy and Moynihan, Congressman O'Neill and Governor Carey, justifying government policy on political prisoners in Northern Ireland and conditions in The Maze prison. (p. 51); 1 May 1979, *Yorkshire Post* (p. 55); 13 May 1983, speech in Perth to Scottish Conservatives (p. 64); 10 October 1986, speech to the Conservative Party Conference (p. 75); 31 December 1979, New Year statement (p. 91); 6 January 1980, interview on ITV's *Weekend World* (p. 96); 31 October 1987, interview published in *Woman's Own* (p. 110); 30 November 1984, TV interview for ITN (p. 137); 8 December 1980, press conference following Anglo-Irish Summit (p. 143); 16 October 1981 Speech at Conservative Party Conference (p. 146); 12 March 1980, Party Political Broadcast (p. 159); 30 December 1979, *News of the World* (p. 166); 25 October 1984, interview for *Birmingham Post* (p. 173); 25 October 1984, interview for *Birmingham Post* (p. 179); 18 May 1983, press conference to launch 1983 Manifesto (p. 183); 16 October 1981, speech to Conservative Party Conference (p. 193); 25 April 1982, on the recapture of South Georgia by British Forces (p. 197); 18 May 1983, Conservative Party Manifesto (p. 206); 19 July 1984, speech to 1922 Committee (Backbench Conservative MPs) (p. 222); 12 October 1984, TV interview outside Lewes police station (p. 234); 12 October 1984, speech to Conservative Party Conference (p. 238); 20 April 1999, a speech at the International Free Enterprise Dinner (p. 241)

ACKNOWLEDGEMENTS

I would like to thank Alan Mahar, Luke Brown and Emma Hargrave at Tindal Street Press for all their work in bringing this novel to publication. Likewise, Hannah Westland, my agent at Rogers, Coleridge & White, for her promotion and support. As always, I would like to thank my family and friends for their love and encouragement of my work.

ABOUT THE AUTHOR

Photo: Richard Battye

Anthony Cartwright was born in Dudley in 1973. He lives in North London with his wife and son.